D1036867

THE MAIDS

THE MAIDS

Junichiro Tanizaki

Translated by Michael P. Cronin

A NEW DIRECTIONS BOOK

Published by arrangement with Chuokoron-Shinsha and the Wylie Agency.

New Directions gratefully acknowledges the support of

Manufactured in the United States of America
New Directions Books are printed on acid-free paper
First published as a New Directions Book in 2017

Library of Congress Cataloging-in-Publication Data
Names: Tanizaki, Jun'ichirō, 1886–1965, author. | Cronin, Michael P. translator.
Title: The maids / Junichiro Tanizaki ; translated by Michael P. Cronin
Other titles: Daidokoro taiheiki. English
Description: First edition. | New York : New Directions Publishing Corporation, 2017. | A New Directions book. | Published as Daidokoro taiheiki in Japanese (Tōkyō : Chūō Kōron Shinsha, 1974).
Identifiers: LCCN 2016037889 | ISBN 9780811224925 (alk. paper)
Subjects: LCSH: Women household employees—Fiction. | Japan—Social life and customs—Fiction. | Japan—Fiction. | Domestic fiction. | Psychological fiction.
Classification: LCC PL839.A7 $B D3513 2017 | DDC 895.63/
LC record available at https://lccn.loc.gov/2016037889

10 9 8 7 6 5 4 3 2 1

New Directions Books are published for James Laughlin
by New Directions Publishing Corporation
80 Eighth Avenue, New York 10011

THE MAIDS

Chapter One

THE WORLD HAS BECOME QUITE COMPLICATED IN recent years. We no longer call the household help "maids," and we can't simply address them by their given names, as we did in the old days—"O-hana," or "O-tama." Now we must say politely, "O-hana-san," "O-tama-san." The Chikura household is rather traditional and followed the old style until recently, but last year, after some criticism, they too started using "-san." I'm sure the current maids will scold me for not following the new etiquette, but it just doesn't feel right, and since this story begins before the war, around 1937, I will call them "maids" and refer to them simply by name, and I beg their indulgence in advance.

I've heard that in some households, even today, they use "Sister" when calling for the maid. Older folks like Raikichi, the master of the Chikura household, hate that practice. These days, you hardly ever see the places we called beef shops, but you used to find them all over Tokyo—places like "Iroha" or "Matsuya," their windows set with red or purple glass. You'd leave your shoes at the entrance, climb some stairs, and enter an enormous room where customers crowded around great simmering pots of sukiyaki. Waitresses dashed among the customers, calling out "Hey, another *sake* for number five!" or "Bill for number seven!" and carrying shoe-check tickets soaked with beef fat. The customers at those places always called the waitresses "Sister" or "Big Sister." That's why, when Raikichi hears someone call for a maid in that way, he can't help but catch a whiff of sukiyaki. He much prefers calling them "O-hana" and "O-tama."

Back in the Meiji era, people called maids by all sorts of demeaning terms. How times have changed! Now some of them object even to "maid-san," and so we're careful to say "helper" or something like that. When addressing maids by name, people today drop the old-fashioned "O" at the beginning and add the more up-to-date "-ko" at the end, to make them "Hanako-san" or "Tamako-san." Raikichi hates that too. He says, "If one is going to use '-san,' then it should be 'Hana-san' and 'Tama-san.' 'Hanako-san' and 'Tamako-san' sound like waitresses, and my house is not a café!" Girls from the provinces who go into service don't understand that way of thinking, though, and they prefer "Hanako-san."

Raikichi set up house with his second wife in the autumn of 1935, when he was fifty and she was thirty-three. I wonder what that place is like nowadays. I understand that it's become part of East Nada ward in Kobe, but back then it was called Tantaka-bayashi, part of the village of Sumiyoshi. Between Sumiyoshi and the town of Uozaki to the east runs the Sumiyoshi River. A bridge, called the Tantaka Bridge, spans it, and the Chikura house stood on the embankment, five or six doors downriver. There were four in the household: the master, Raikichi; his wife, Sanko; her seven-year-old daughter by a former marriage, Mutsuko, whom Raikichi would later adopt; and the wife's younger sister, Nioko. And then there were always several maids—at least two or three and sometimes as many as five or six.

You might think there was no need to employ so many maids for a household of women (except Raikichi), but these were pampered young ladies who had grown up in luxury, and they couldn't have managed without at least that many servants. Besides, Raikichi liked to have a lot of maids around—he said it made the house bright and lively. As a result, many, many maids have worked for the Chikura household over the years. From Tantaka-bayashi the family moved across the river to Uozaki and then, when the war began, they fled east to a country villa in Atami, in Shizuoka prefecture. After the war, they split their time between that villa and a house in Kyoto, and the number of maids multiplied—the wife, Sanko, was a soft touch, the sort who would take on any number of girls if asked to.

So I really couldn't count the number of girls who helped out in the kitchens of the Chikura household before the move to Atami. Some worked there for less than a month, while others stayed six, seven, even ten years or more. Whenever Raikichi meets a girl who was with the family for a long time, he treats her just as affectionately as he would his own daughter. He even let some of the young maids who were far from their hometowns hold their engagement ceremonies at the house. A few who married and settled nearby still drop by to visit from time to time. It's just as they say: "Close strangers are better than distant family."

But however many servants the family has employed over the years, almost all of the maids have been Kansai girls, from the west country. Two or three years ago, for the first time, we did have a girl come to us from Ibaraki, but she soon quit and returned to her hometown, and right now we have a girl from here in Shizuoka, born at the foot of Mount Fuji, but we haven't had any other girls from the east. I suppose it's natural. Sanko is from Osaka, after all, and the family's first house was on the Hanshin Railway line between Osaka and Kobe. After the war, they moved from the Osaka-Kobe region to Kyoto, and now they've left Kyoto for good and set up house here in Atami. Still, Raikichi's wife and her family dislike the rough manners of girls from the east, around Tokyo, and, when they come to hire a new maid, they always look for a girl from the west. This Atami house is in Narusawa, near Izusan. Here, as they come in and out of the kitchen, the deliverymen from the grocer's and the fish market speak in a brisk Tokyo patter, but the maids reply in the Osaka dialect. After all, the whole family speak in dialect, and these girls from the Kansai countryside have no chance to learn the smooth, clipped Tokyo way of speaking. So they stick to their Osaka ways; they even slice pickled radish in sticks, Osaka-style, not rounds.

Raikichi is originally from Tokyo but, in the twenty-odd years since he married his present wife, he has been living in a house where everyone else prattles on from morning till night in the Osaka dialect until at last, influenced by these surroundings, he has developed a strange manner of speech and forgotten his native tongue. Talking with people from Tokyo, he'll inadvertently use the Osaka word *hokasu* instead of *suteru* for "throw away," and be ridiculed for it. Between husband and wife, too, silly little quarrels sometimes arise over differences in customs and habits, but his wife has her daughter and younger sister to back her up, so if the quarrel escalates, Raikichi just surrenders.

The west-country maids, when they move here to Atami, begin to mimic the deliverymen who come and go, and they pick up various Tokyo expressions—if only the words and not the intonation. At the grocer's, they have different names for everything: ginger is *hine-shōga,* rather than *tsuchi-shōga*; Mizuna greens they call *Kyō-na*; and taro is *sato-imo*, not *ko-imo*. What we call *ito-konnyaku* noodles they call *shirataki* and vice versa; and pumpkin is *tōnasu*, not *nankin*. At the fishmonger's, too, everything is called something else. The girls can't get their shopping done if they don't use the Tokyo names for things, so they learn the words they need to get by, but they could never lose their accent. They still use many Kansai expressions without the slightest hesitation. In the past, people would be embarrassed to use the Kansai dialect in the middle of Tokyo, but these days, Osaka comedy teams come to Tokyo on tour, and they're all over the movies too. Even the deliverymen have caught the fever for Osaka words, saying *Nanbo?* instead of *Ikura?* for "How much?" and *Ookini,* not *Arigatō,* for "Thank you."

Now then, from here on, I am going to select from among all the maids who've worked in the Chikura household—from the days in Tantaka-bayashi until the move to Atami—a few who, for various reasons, made an unforgettable impression. I want to lay them out on the cutting board, as it were, and record my memories of them. I'll try to describe them accurately but, after all, my intention is to produce a novel, so I may embroider things a little. Please bear this in mind; it would be a terrible insult to Raikichi and to the people who served as models for the other characters if you were to take the events recorded here as exactly true from start to finish.

I wrote that Raikichi and Sanko made their first home in Tantaka-bayashi, but in fact they lived together secretly before that, at a place in Ashiya with a fake name on the door. That has nothing to do with the present story, though, so we'll ignore it. There were maids at that Ashiya house, but the first to come into service at Tantaka-bayashi, after the couple decided to live together openly, was a girl from Kagoshima named Hatsu. Her name means "First," so let's begin our story there.

Raikichi has never set foot in Kagoshima, and he knows little about its geography, but every year, when typhoons strike the Kyushu area, Makurazaki city in Kagoshima invariably appears in the newspapers. The map shows Makurazaki situated near the southern tip of Kyushu, and notes a lighthouse. Hatsu was born just outside Makurazaki, in the village of Nishi-minamikata, in Kawanabe county (now the town of Bōnotsu). Her family made their living there farming and fishing, she said.

Hatsu came to the household in the summer of 1936. Two girls named Haru and Mitsu had been working there for some time, but it was decided that one more maid was needed. Hatsu came recommended by one of Sanko's friends, the wife of a dentist. She was twenty years old, and had worked briefly in two or three houses in Kobe. "Hatsu" was not her real name; that was Sakihana Wakae. In Sanko's family—an old, established one in Osaka—it was customary to give a maid a new name for service, since using her real name was considered an insult to the girl's parents. When this new girl arrived, everyone discussed what to call her and decided "'Hatsu' will do."

I don't know how long she had been in service in Kobe, but Hatsu was not very sophisticated when she arrived at the Chikura household. Presenting herself to the master and his wife for the first time, she prostrated herself in the front hall, pressing her forehead against the wooden floor.

"Where in Kobe were you working before coming here?" Sanko asked her.

"In Nunobiki, ma'am."

"And how long were you working there?"

"About two weeks."

"Why did you leave after just two weeks?" But when Sanko asked this, Hatsu only smirked. "Did the master let you go?"

"No, ma'am, it wasn't like that."

"You quit, then?"

"Yes, ma'am."

"For what reason?"

But Hatsu just kept smirking, and wouldn't give a reason.

Sanko and Raikichi didn't suppose the circumstances could be particularly serious and so they left it there. But two or three days later, one of the other maids, Haru, went to Sanko and the other ladies and said she had heard the reason. According to her, the master of the Kobe house had forced himself on Hatsu, and she had run away.

"Really!" Sanko said, turning to the other ladies, "That girl?" Hatsu was quite plain, you see; no one would call her pretty, even in flattery. She herself admitted as much. At the house where she was in service before Nunobiki, she said, the son had teased her day in and day out about her looks, especially her broad, flat nose. He would say to her, "With that flat nose, you could fall down face-first and not hurt it!" He teased her so relentlessly that she thought to herself, "I can't take it! I just can't take it!"

One day soon after she came to the Chikura household, Hatsu came flying out of the kitchen and into the parlor crying "Madam!" (she used an old-fashioned Osaka style of address, as the whole household did until the end of the war): "Madam! It's true!"

When Sanko asked, "What's true?" Hatsu, rubbing her cheeks, responded:

"Sure enough, what that boy said is true!" It turned out that Hatsu had slipped on the threshold of the earthen-floored kitchen and landed with her face in the dirt. She had scraped her cheeks, but hadn't hurt her nose at all. And she had seen fit to come and report this to Madam!

All this brings to mind *Gone With the Wind*, and the black maid played by Hattie McDaniel (although the movie showed in Japan well after this episode, of course); the mistress's daughter, Mutsuko, used to say that whenever she looked at McDaniel, Hatsu's face would float before her eyes like a double exposure.

Chapter Two

SURE ENOUGH, WITH HER FULL CHEEKS, ROUND
face, wide mouth, and strong jaw, Hatsu did resemble McDaniel; and
yet there was something rather winsome in her round eyes. Besides,
her teeth were extraordinarily white and straight, and whenever she
spoke, one could see them, wet and glistening.

Hatsu's best feature was not her face, but her figure. When Mutsuko compared her to McDaniel, she was thinking only of the shape
of her face; her skin was snow white. Her figure was ample and well
developed, but not sloppy. She was taller than average for a twenty-
year-old woman of that time, almost thirty years ago, and fit. Her
fingers were long, and her feet, though quite big, were not badly
shaped. And though Raikichi hadn't seen her naked, according to
Mutsuko her bust was "better than Marilyn Monroe's."

Most maids didn't begin to wear western-style clothes until after the war; at the time of this story, they still wore kimono. Once,
though, on her day off, Hatsu dressed up in fancy western-style
clothes—the sort of thing that only fashionable types wore back

then—and went off somewhere. As Raikichi looked down from a second-floor window to watch her leaving, he was struck by the symmetry of her limbs. Her shoulders, arms, and breasts were nicely rounded; her legs were pleasingly plump and perfectly straight; and her feet looked splendid in western shoes. She always displayed admirable neatness and modesty, and she kept herself very clean. Raikichi hated to see a woman with dirty soles, and the soles of Hatsu's feet always looked smooth and pure white, as though she had just scrubbed them with a washcloth. If you happened to peer down into her collar, you'd find her underclothes freshly washed and impeccably clean. This always led Raikichi to think that, even though her face was plain, as tall as she was and with a body like that, Hatsu would probably be ten or twenty times as attractive as she was now if only she had been born into a good family in the city and raised with some sense of how to dress and make herself up. For that matter, even her eyes—if she had at least graduated from a girls' school—might have been enlivened by a spark of intelligence to lend her features a certain charm. Whenever this occurred to him, he felt sorry that Hatsu had been born in a poor fishing village on the distant shore of Kyushu.

Time passed and one day—was it just a year after Hatsu came to us?—a cousin of Hatsu's called Etsu trundled up to the Chikura house carrying a wicker trunk. This girl hadn't just arrived from Kagoshima; she had been in service at some house in Sumiyoshi, not far off, but, bullied by the daughter there, she had run away and eventually dragged herself over here and landed with us. Etsu wasn't as tall as Hatsu; she was rather short and stout. She had no special feature you could point to, but, like Hatsu, she was honest and sincere. In keeping with her impressive physique, Hatsu had a generous, take-charge quality, and the other girls from her hometown looked up to her like a big sister. It wasn't just Etsu—girls came one after another from Tomari to stay with us. Some traveled all the way from Kyushu with no particular destination in mind and set their bags down in

Hatsu's room for a while. Others were in service in the Osaka-Kobe region but didn't like where they were working and stopped in to consult Hatsu about their direction in life. Hatsu took any number of such girls under her wing and let them stay with her in the maids' room—and since the family couldn't simply ignore them, they had to consider each case and help guide the girls in the proper direction. At times there would be three or four girls staying in the room with Hatsu and not enough bedding for all of them, but Hatsu, generous to a fault, would nonchalantly set out the mattresses meant for houseguests. Sanko was dumbfounded each time she did it.

I've called it the maids' room, but it was only four and half mats in size, or about seventy-five square feet. Often, there were seven or eight girls sleeping in there, crammed together like sardines. You can't imagine the noise. The more senior maids, Haru and Mitsu, would be almost pushed out of the room—pressed up against the wall, their legs splaying into the hallway—while the other girls from her village clustered around Hatsu, jabbering away in their incomprehensible Kagoshima dialect, so that you'd swear you were in a bustling fish market in Makurazaki. Raikichi called these gatherings in the maids' room "the Kagoshima Prefectural Association." Needless to say, Hatsu always took the lead. The others in the group seemed to defer to her, falling in line with whatever she suggested.

They would never disagree with Hatsu—they had come to rely on her. This was characteristic of Kagoshima; it seems that people there haven't yet outgrown the feudal mindset; they submit to their elders, even if the age difference is only one year. The old folk there consider it an admirable local custom. Hatsu was clearly the eldest of the girls; all of the others were about sixteen or seventeen, eighteen or nineteen, which made Hatsu all the more high-handed.

At the time, there was a driving range at a place called Aogi,* between the Fukae and Uozaki stations on the Hanshin Line, and

---

* Now called Ōgi.

sometimes a young golf pro named Nitta who worked there would visit the Chikura house, chatting with Sanko and Nioko or taking Mutsuko to the nearby beach. One summer night after ten, unaware that the whole family had gone out to cool off, this Nitta entered the house through the kitchen to find the door to the maids' quarters wide open and the electric light left on, burning bright, and the "Prefectural Association" asleep and snoring loudly, exhausted from all their talk. Among them was Hatsu, stretched out on top of the female bodies that were piled up like soft white rice cakes, her magnificent breasts—better than Monroe's—bare, so that he could not help but see. Shocked, Nitta started to run away, but—Wait! Wait!—realizing that he would certainly never again see such an amazing "nude show," he changed his mind and returned. Taking out a camera that, by luck, he happened to have with him and shoving aside the piled-up thighs, he pulled the sleeping Hatsu out and patiently, from left and right, assiduously took photo after photo of her.

The next day, after developing the film, he showed the negatives to Sanko, saying "Madam, I've got something good to show you!"

"When did you take these?!" Sanko said. "I can't have such pranks!" And with that she hastily seized the negatives. As a result, Raikichi never got to see them, but according to Sanko, Hatsu's body was even more seductive in photos.

When Hatsu spoke with anyone in the family, she could manage a perfunctory sort of Kansai style, but when she fell into conversation with friends from her home prefecture, she would break into her bizarre native dialect, and family members close enough to hear would have no idea at all what she was saying. Little Mutsuko, however, was always going to the maids' quarters to make friends and play with the women there so that, little by little, she learned their dialect and eventually she could understand everything they said. The following vocabulary list will give you some idea; it's a sample taken from a dialect dictionary that Mutsuko wrote down for her mother and the other ladies:

	HATSU'S DIALECT	STANDARD JAPANESE
How are you?	*Genki yaiko*	*Genki desu ka*
What shall I do?!	*Ikensui mon ka*	*Dō shitara ii darō ka*
Please	*Kuremekko*	*Kudasai*
Terribly	*gattsui*	*taihen*
White radish	*dekon*	*daikon*
Carrot	*nijin*	*ninjin*
Really, truly	*Hon no kochi*	*Hontō ni*
Sincerely	*Makotē*	*Makoto ni*
What are you saying?	*Nai iwattoko*	*Nani o itte iru no desu ka*
What are you doing?	*Nai serattoko*	*Nani o shite iru no desu ka*
Myself	*oi*	*jibun*
You	*akko*	*omae*
To sleep	*nuddo*	*neru*
Come here!	*Kimecchō*	*Kinasai yo*
Where are you going?	*Dokē ikakko*	*Doko e iku no desu ka*
Isn't that good news!	*Yoka hanajjarai*	*Ii hanashi da nā*

People speak of "the jabbering of southern barbarians," and the maids' dialect was exactly that; far stranger than English or French. When it's transcribed, you can more or less guess the meaning, but spoken fast and with an accent, there was absolutely no understanding it.

One day, Raikichi was quarreling with his wife, and Hatsu, sympathizing with Sanko, said *Ikketsun mo naka jijikko,* intentionally using her Kagoshima dialect. Mutsuko informed them that this translated to *Ikesukanai jīsan,* or "What a mean old man!"

Kuremekko, or "please," was a word they all learned and adopted enthusiastically, saying, "Bring the tea, *kuremekko,*" or "Serve dinner, *kuremekko.*"

When speaking the Kansai dialect with the family, Hatsu would occasionally use a strange intonation or mix up accents. She would transpose syllables, so that, for example, the word for body, *karada,* became *kadara*; even when corrected, she somehow couldn't say *karada.* She also mispronounced *da* as *ra,* so a phrase like *yodare ga daradara* ("drooling saliva") became *yorare ga rarara.* When she tried to mimic the Tokyo dialect and say *shichatta* ("I've gone and done it"), it came out backwards, as *shitaccha.* On top of all this, when something surprised her, she would shout *Taa!* in an extraordinary voice. It wasn't just Hatsu; all the girls from her prefecture did the same.

Earlier, I mentioned another maid, called Etsu. Their pronunciation of this name, too, was somehow different from the usual pronunciation. They said the first syllable as "ye" and gave it a strong accent, so it sounded like *Yay*-tsu. Several of the other girls had unfamiliar-sounding names, too. For instance, one was called Fuko. I suppose this was a mispronunciation of Fuku, but I dare say it's written down as Fuko even in the family register. Those are two of the simpler ones. There were others with names like Esu, Tsumi, Yotsu, Ezu, Rito, Kie, and so on—I can't even guess how to write them in *kanji* characters.

Although Hatsu, with her grand presence, affected the pose of a big sister to the other girls from her province, she was really very timid and fainthearted. When, occasionally, a pushy salesman or a beggar would get into the house through the back door, she would turn pale and tremble like a leaf. She shook so badly, you could actually hear her teeth chattering. One time—when was it?—she charged into the kitchen saying "There's an *apa* beggar here!" and, crying, *Apa! Apa!* she passed out. It caused quite an uproar. It turned out that *apa* is Kagoshima dialect for "mute," but I don't know why a mute beggar should be so terrifying.

Yes, despite her physique, Hatsu was extremely high-strung. In particular, she had a terror of contracting tuberculosis. It seems that, in her hometown, once someone comes down with tuberculosis, no one will associate with them. If someone is found to be infected, the family sets up a hut on the other side of the mountain and takes the sick person there. Not even the parents and siblings go near except to bring food. For this reason, the idea of falling ill frightened Hatsu more than anything else. One of her brothers had already died of lung disease and another was confined to bed with TB, so it was understandable that Hatsu was highly anxious. If she felt a little under the weather, she immediately became convinced that she had contracted tuberculosis and would go off by herself to brood. At such times, no matter what the members of the family said to her, she wouldn't reply but would only pout, her face like a puffer-fish lantern. Sanko would say to her, "What's wrong with your face? Just take a look at yourself in the mirror."

She pouted like this so often that at last Sanko became fed up and said to her, "I have no use for someone like you. Go back home!"

With that, Hatsu said, "Okay, I'll go," and went off meekly. But she returned before long. This happened two or three times, I'm sure.

Chapter Three

BEFORE THE TUNNEL OPENED BETWEEN SHIMONO-
seki and Moji, in Kita-Kyushu, the trip Hatsu made from her hometown to Sumiyoshi, in Kansai, took much longer than it does now.
First of all, it was about four miles from her village, Tomari, to the
terminal of the private Nansatsu train line in Makurazaki. A bus ran
between them, but Haru usually walked. Then, she took the Nansatsu line from Makurazaki to Ijūin, where she changed to the national railway. Later, they started running a diesel train on that route,
but back then it was a steam locomotive, and the trip took two hours.
At Ijūin, she could catch the express train coming from Kagoshima
and take that to Kobe, but the leg from Ijūin to Moji took nine hours
and thirty minutes, and then there was a ten-minute wait for the
ferry, a fifteen-minute ferry ride, and a thirty-five-minute wait for
the train at Shimonoseki. Then the trip from Shimonoseki to Kobe
took ten hours and thirteen minutes, so the entire trip from Makurazaki took twenty-two hours and forty-three minutes. To make
matters worse, there were seldom seats available for those boarding

at Ijūin, so Haru often had to stand until Hiroshima. Finally, she had to change trains at Sannomiya Station in Kobe, and it took another twenty-five or twenty-six minutes before she arrived in Sumiyoshi. The train fare in those days was about ten yen. For someone like Hatsu—a naive country girl who had rarely traveled even as far as Kagoshima City, next door, and had never been to Ibusuki, the famous nearby hot spring—it was a tremendous journey. Hatsu didn't travel well and would eat almost nothing on the train. Though she was a big woman, she was wilting with exhaustion by the time she arrived at Sumiyoshi and would fall dead asleep for a full night and day.

Hatsu had moped off after being told "I have no use for you; go back home." When she returned six months later, Sanko asked her, "What were you doing back home?"

She responded, "I was helping my mother with the farming and fishing, ma'am."

"What about your father?" Sanko asked.

"He passed away, ma'am."

I've already noted that she had two brothers, one who died and another bedridden with tuberculosis. Sanko asked if she had other siblings.

"I have one younger sister."

"And what does she do?"

"She lives in Wakayama, in the Kishū domain" (as it was then called).

"What is she doing in Wakayama? Did she marry someone from there?"

"No, ma'am" she answered. "She's in service there."

"How old is she?"

"She's twenty-six."

"And why did she go all the way to Wakayama, of all places?"

Hatsu tried to conceal the reason at first. "She went there last year, ma'am."

As Sanko questioned her more closely, it came out, though not in so many words, that her sister had been indentured to someone in Wakayama. Five years earlier, the sister had left their hometown and gone to Kobe, where at first she worked in a respectable house. Her family was poor, though, and debts had piled up during her father's lifetime, so she was pressured to send money back to them each month. She became a live-in servant for a family that had advanced her family three thousand yen, and a downward spiral carried her to Wakayama.

"Do you have any other siblings?"

"One younger brother, ma'am."

"And how old is he?"

Her younger brother was seventeen, and had been working on a fishing boat since the previous year.

Life had not been easy at all for Haru after she returned to her hometown. She had submitted to hard labor from morning to night, in the fields and on the shore, to help her aging mother. At Tantakabayashi, she could eat white rice three times a day, but at her mother's house they had to make do with yams. She had grown thin, her eyes sunken, her cheekbones sharper. Her skin, once so white, had in that short time become sunburnt to a dark sepia. Her already plain face had become a degree uglier, so that she returned as the type of woman to whom no one would give a second glance.

"Just look how changed her face is!" said the members of the Chikura household. At the time, they felt both pity and wonder as they stared at Hatsu, who had, in such a short time, changed so much as to seem a stranger. Surprisingly, though, as one month passed and then another, her sunburn faded, her face and body filled out, and soon she was again her old fair, full-figured self. Sanko and the others were shocked to learn what a transformation circumstances and climate could work on a woman.

"You must've had no fun at all back at your mother's house, working all day till you were burnt to a crisp."

"No, ma'am, I didn't."

"Is everyone there so busy—men and women both?"

"Yes, ma'am."

"But isn't there any fun at all to be had?"

"Some people have their fun," Hatsu said.

There is not a single man in that part of the country that does not engage in "night-crawling," that is, clandestine visits to unmarried women living with their parents. There they call it "night-talk" and the men who do it "night-talkers," and all the women there put up with it. Marriage there is called *goze-muke* or "receiving a wife," and they have long followed a custom of letting couples live together provisionally beforehand; if the woman meets with the man's approval, they marry formally and, if not, he sends her back to her family. They call this provisional marriage *ashi-ire*, or "putting one's foot in," and it's not limited to Hatsu's hometown, but is practiced in areas all over Japan. If she is rejected by a man, the woman returns to her parents' house without a second thought. It's accepted as natural, and her parents do not reprimand her. In this way, both men and women try out various partners until they find one they like.

"Hatsu, did you have men visit you for 'night-talk' too?"

"No, ma'am, not me. I was about the only one in my village who was never visited."

"Good for you! Not even once?"

"No, but once I kicked a man out of my house."

So Hatsu declared, but this was nothing to be proud of; it only meant that she was considered too ugly in her village.

The Chikura house in Tantaka-bayashi was set on the bank of the Sumiyoshi River. The front gate was on the east side of the house, facing the river, and the back gate was on the west side, opposite the Furushinden neighborhood. Tradesmen would enter through the back gate and look in at the kitchen door. Just outside it was a well with a motorized pump and the men would gather there whenever they had a free moment to flirt with the maids. Before long, Hatsu became friendly with a repairman from Kansai Electric named

Terada. Whenever a fuse blew or the electric iron stopped working, she would call this man and he would immediately dash over, and soon they would be tucked away over by the well, deep in conversation. Sanko was comparatively liberal with the help and, if anything, too patient. She was looking after other women's daughters, so it wouldn't do to make any mistakes, but it was her principle to tolerate such friendships, and soon two or three more young men from Kansai Electric were accompanying Terada on his visits. Eventually, Etsu, Haru, and Mitsu all had boyfriends from Kansai Electric. Late at night, after the family had gone to bed, the maids would place phone calls to their boyfriends and, whispering into the receiver, lose themselves in intimate conversations—Mutsuko once found the bell wrapped in paper to silence it.

However—while I don't mean to defend Sanko here—neither Hatsu nor the other girls ever got into real trouble, even when out of the master's sight. Sanko had announced to the girls: "All of you are of marriageable age, so if you meet someone you like, I prefer you to tell me rather than concealing it. I won't restrict you from seeing a man unless I have a good reason. However, sometimes girls are deceived by unscrupulous men, so if, after a certain period of association, you determine *This is the one for me*, I will meet with him myself and then communicate with your family back home and, depending on how matters proceed, even stand as go-between at your wedding. To this extent, you are free to socialize as you wish, but you must not form more serious attachments."

The maids believed Sanko, and Sanko trusted the maids, and as far as Raikichi could tell, neither side had betrayed that trust. Not that there weren't one or two exceptions among all the people they employed over the years, but in general the maids had depended on Sanko's liberal nature without taking advantage of it.

Hatsu came to the Sumiyoshi house in 1936, a year before the Marco Polo Bridge Incident that started the second Sino-Japanese War. Who knows how Hatsu's relationship with Terada might have developed if it hadn't been for that incident. Perhaps the other girls, too, would have made good matches with their boyfriends. The world was changing, though, and no longer the place for such matters. In the end, none of those relationships survived. Over the next two years, the boyfriends were drafted one by one and went off to war. Every household suffered from a shortage of help as maids returned to their hometowns. Thanks to Haru, however, the Chikura household could still beckon any number of girls from Kagoshima. Far from being inconvenienced, they had so much extra help that they could send girls out to lend a hand at their friends' houses.

Now that I think of it, there was a novelist, Mr. Kiga, who had moved from Nara to Tokyo and had taken a house in the neighborhood of Takadanobaba.* He was having trouble finding a maid, so we sent a girl named Sato to help him. This girl had been at the Chikura house only a very short time. She had good features and striking eyes—I suppose she was one of the most beautiful girls to work in the Chikura household. I heard that she was highly valued at the Kiga house for her clever ways and helpful attitude and worked there until the beginning of the Greater East Asian War, when she returned to her hometown. Haru, who began at the Chikura house before Hatsu, also asked for time off when the war began; she returned to her parents' home in Amagasaki and was married before long. Her husband was called up too.

Mindful of the possibility of air raids in the Osaka-Kobe region, the Chikura family secured a small villa in the Nishiyama area of Atami in April of 1942 to use as a shelter if one should become necessary. Occasionally they made the trip from Sumiyoshi there and back. Raikichi stayed there for the first time at the beginning of April. At first, he didn't take the family with him, but traveled with

---

* Kiga is presumably a stand-in for the author Shiga Naoya, who moved from Nara to Takadanobaba in Tokyo in 1938.—Tr.

only Hatsu. They went just to see how comfortable it was. This was at the time of the first US air raid, when Doolittle's planes assaulted the skies over Tokyo and escaped, though without any great success. The planes didn't pass over Atami, but the news that "Tokyo has been hit!" caused a furor.

Raikichi took Hatsu with him because he liked her best of the three or four maids then at the house. He liked her, first of all, because, as I said earlier, she was neat and clean. Though her face was homely, her figure was statuesque, her skin fair, her hands and feet long and lissome, and she inspired no sense of discomfort in Raikichi. Second, she was almost neurotically conscientious about financial matters, so he could relax and depend on her to handle all the accounting. It wasn't that the other maids were careless, of course, but only Hatsu would calculate every expense down to one one-hundredth of a yen, recording them all in a notebook in her poor handwriting. Third—and this was the most important point—she was the best cook among the maids. Not only Hatsu, but all the girls from Kagoshima demonstrated great skill in seasoning. Perhaps you could call it a special characteristic of people from that region. Girls born there, even rubes fresh from the countryside, had an unusually well-developed sense of taste. If asked to season some dish, none of them would ever go very wrong and spoil the flavor. But Hatsu excelled them all in making simmered or broiled dishes, or broth for soup. When asked to prepare even a simple sesame dressing or tofu salad, the result was exceptionally delicious. Her best dish, though, was tempura. She would vigorously fill a pot with oil and briskly light the coals in the range. Sanko would caution her every time, "Careful! Careful! What if the flames catch on the oil?" But Hatsu ignored her and maintained her composure. She would boldly add oil to the pot and coal to the fire until the whole kitchen seemed to be ablaze, what with the smoke from the oil and the red of the fire reflected in the paper screens, but she'd continue to fry the tempura, unflustered, whether through confidence in her own skill or pure recklessness.

Around that time, food supplies in the Hanshin region were getting scarcer every day, but they were still relatively plentiful in the special resort towns of Atami and Karuizawa. Every day, that glutton Raikichi would urge Hatsu to lock up the villa and walk down the Nishiyama slope to town to search for something good to eat. One time, finding fresh *wakame* seaweed at a greengrocers, Raikichi called out, "Hatsu! Let's buy that!" and had her bring it home and serve it with soy sauce and vinegar. Even today, Raikichi can't forget the delicious taste of that fresh *wakame*.

Hatsu was impressed, too. "You can get everything in Atami, can't you, sir!" she would say as she stopped at a storefront, opened her shopping basket, and eagerly loaded it. Hatsu's hometown was apparently near fishing grounds for yellowtail and bonito. Although it was not yet the season, winter yellowtail were being caught at Atami in great numbers. No matter how many were caught, though, this was before they could be shipped to Tokyo, so one sometimes saw people walking through town dragging fresh yellowtail, blood dripping, on a rope.

Chapter Four

HATSU WAS AN EXCELLENT JUDGE OF FISH. IF RAIKI-
chi told her, "Get that one," she wouldn't buy it immediately but
would spread open the gills before declaring, "this one is old," or "this
one is fit to eat." Raised in a fishing village, she said that a slightly
off fish that smelled of the sea appealed to her more than one that
was too fresh.

The Atami of today is a product of the postwar era. At that time,
there was not a single proper house on the reclaimed land along the
coast, and the plaza there was just a field where children played catch
and the town's young men marched and drilled. On the main shopping street, before the Great Fire of 1950, there remained traces of the
old Meiji-era hot-spring resort. The famous O-Miya pine tree that
today is surrounded by busy streets stood on a lonely wave-swept
shore in those days, and the nearby stone slab inscribed with Oguri
Fūyō's haiku — "Just like O-Miya was the retreating figure beneath a
spring moon" — was buffeted by salty sea breezes.

"Hatsu, what sort of place is your hometown? It must be quite different from here."

"No, sir, in fact it's quite similar." She said that the topography of Atami, with the mountain lurking in the background, the merest plain in the middle distance, and, in the foreground, the bay, was exactly like Tomari. The moment she stepped off the train, she had thought of her hometown.

"Bōnotsu's countless rooftops are hidden by the sails of countless ships departing"—so goes an old folk song about Hatsu's hometown, Tomari, otherwise known as Bōnotsu, which was apparently a thriving port until Nagasaki was opened to trade. In ancient times, envoys from Tang China arrived and departed there; indeed, at one time it was called the Tang Port. It gradually declined into a modest fishing village but, Hatsu said, Atami could not match the magnificence of its scenery. In Atami, places like the particolored cliffs of Nishikigaura are counted as famous sights, but Bōnotsu had many spots just as beautiful; the eight famous sites of Bōnotsu, Ear-Pull Pass, the twin sword stones in the bay—all were as pretty as pictures. While there were many clementine and bitter-orange trees here in Atami, ponkan oranges and mandarins grew in terraced rows on the mountains behind Tomari. The climate was warm there, and the gentle touch of the air on your skin, the color of the sea, the movement of the clouds, the echo of the waves—all of it was quite like here in Atami, Hatsu said.

In April of 1941, the year before Raikichi took the villa in Atami, his sister-in-law, Sanko's younger sister, Nioko, had married into the noble Asukai family and moved from Sumiyoshi to a house in Tokyo near Yūtenji Station on the Tōyoko Line. After that, she got into the habit of going to Atami to get together with Sanko, but if Nioko wasn't visiting, Sanko didn't much like traveling to the Kanto region, and spent more of her time in Sumiyoshi until the war worsened in 1942 and 1943.

Raikichi appended a modest poem to a letter he sent his wife on New Year's Day of 1944:

Come, nightingale, quickly, quickly! Here at Nishiyama
In my little garden, now the plum is blooming!

Still, Sanko hesitated. And if she did go out to Atami, she would not stay, but would either go on to Tokyo for some entertainment there or return to Sumiyoshi directly. Naturally, Raikichi often made the trip back and forth to Sumiyoshi, but he spent many nights at Nishiyama, with Hatsu.

Military censors were keeping a close watch on the novel Raikichi was writing. Even if he did finish it, no one would be willing to publish the book, and so, with nothing to fill his time, all he could do was listen to the radio or play the gramophone or, failing that, go out and try to rustle up some provisions. That he could live this way without succumbing to the tedium was no doubt thanks to the delicious meals that Hatsu prepared for him each day. When the weather was fine, Raikichi would take a wicker chair out to the lawn and have Hatsu trim his hair. Impatient by nature, Raikichi hated being made to wait at a barbershop and had always gotten his hair trimmed at home, but Hatsu had assumed exclusive responsibility for barbering after she arrived. Raikichi had her do it not with electric clippers but with scissors—snip, snip—and although she scalped him the first time, she gradually grew more proficient until she could trim his hair quite expertly. Sometimes they would spend the whole day out there together, weeding and mowing the lawn.

I don't know what Hatsu thought of Raikichi, but once, when Raikichi came to the maids' room in the middle of the night to wake her up for some reason, he found the sliding screen firmly wedged shut with a stick (Hatsu hadn't made the stick herself; it had been there before). Once he woke her, Hatsu removed the stick and came out in her nightclothes; still, it seems she took some precautions against Raikichi. That was the only time he came to wake her in the middle of the night, so I don't know if she was always so careful.

It was around the fall of 1944, wasn't it, when Hatsu, who had arrived in 1936, was summoned back to her hometown because her mother was sick. She was twenty when she arrived in Sumiyoshi, and she worked there for nearly nine years, so she must have been about twenty-eight when she left. Two or three days before her departure, Raikichi asked her to give him a "farewell-for-now" haircut. That day, somehow, the war seemed far away. The weather was glorious and calm, and the impression still lingers of seeing Hatsu's face with distinct clarity, bathed in the garden's afternoon sunlight, and hearing the brisk snip-snip of the scissors.

"Come back when the war has ended."

"Yes, sir. I'll come back." With those words, Hatsu departed from Kinomiya Station, bright and cheerful, unsentimental to the last. Raikichi saw her off and wrote this poem to commemorate the occasion:

> *Even as you fish on the beach at Tomari by Satsuma Bay*
> *See that you do not forget the warm waters of Izu.*

In April of that year, Sanko and Mutsuko moved to Atami, and Mutsuko transferred from Kōnan Girls School to Itō Girls School. The previous year, they had vacated the Sumiyoshi house and moved across the river to Uozaki. They left this house in the care of Sanko's second younger sister, Inoue Teruko, and a cousin, Shimada, and his family. Of the once lively "Kagoshima Prefectural Association," not a single girl remained. Hatsu had been the first to arrive and had worked there until the end. Her cousin Etsu left just before her to marry a man in Kyushu. She, too, was a devoted servant, and threw herself into her work. In summer, when Etsu was left on her own at the Nishiyama villa, she said she couldn't stand being idle, and surprised us by clearing the garden of weeds until not a single stray leaf remained. After the war ended, she came with her children to visit the family in Kyoto, but that was a long time ago, and we haven't had any word of her since.

Hatsu spent only two years back in her hometown. After the war, in the spring of 1946, just before the dispersal of the Chikura household, she came to an inn at Katsuyama, in Okayama, and was with the family as they moved to Kyoto, staying first at Nanzenji temple and then the Shimogamo Shrine. That's another long story, though, so for now I'll end Hatsu's wartime chapter here. One way and another, the family persevered at Atami through 1943; even with flounder selling for 100 yen each, they could enjoy small luxuries. But by the following year, that was no longer possible, and there was no way for Hatsu to exert her skills in the kitchen. During the time she was in Atami, straw men were set up for bayonet practice in front of the reservoir near that famous eel restaurant, Jūbako, and even girls were made to participate, using bamboo spears. Two or three times, Hatsu was rounded up and made to join the drills. On top of that, after she returned to Tomari, she had to do all the work herself while nursing her sick mother and her bedridden little brother; so we can suppose that she suffered more than her share. Yet, to her credit, she found time to write Raikichi and his wife from time to time. I have here one of Hatsu's letters—from 1945, apparently; I'll reprint it so you can have a look.

Dear Madam,

Thank you very much for going to the trouble of sending me a package the other day. It must have been a great nuisance for you and I cannot find words to express my gratitude that Sensei and Madam should show such kindness to someone like me. I deeply regret to inform you that the package was apparently opened and the contents stolen. When I received it only two namako (sea cucumbers) were ??? It was so very regrettable I could of (sic) wept. I was about to write to thank you in a timely fashion when I had to go to Kumamoto on the twentieth to barter some salt for rice and so I am writing only now and I do humbly beg your pardon. These days it is very usual for people to go to Kumamoto or to Saga to barter for rice. Usually people take salt, clothing, etc. On the twelfth, I trudged ten miles down the road to the station, carried a trunk full of salt (three and a half gallons) on my back then got in line to buy a ticket, stayed up all night, and caught a train the next day. I was able to exchange the salt for an equal amount of rice, but the trip home was a terrible hardship, the train very crowded with demobilized soldiers and other folks returning with bartered rice. Every day, seventy or eighty people from villages all over gather at Kumamoto Station to barter for rice. I finally reached Matsurazaki Station a little after nine in the evening. I then walked the ten miles back again, this time carrying three and a half gallons of rice, and got home just after midnight. As I rode the train and walked that road I thought to myself, Must I suffer so much just to eat? But my mother and my big brother beamed with happiness when they saw the snow-white grains of rice, and I was so happy that all my troubles flew away. Thankfully, we were able to eat our fill. Some unlucky folks go to all the trouble of bartering for rice and carrying it back home only to have it confiscated by the police, but we have been luckier. My little brother has not returned from Taiwan yet, though some soldiers are making their way back, but the whole family was relieved when at last we had a postcard from him on the fourteenth saying that he is doing his duty cheerfully. In closing, please convey my regards to Miss Nioko and the young miss.

Sincerely, Hatsu

I have reproduced Hatsu's letter here exactly, without correcting a single sentence or word. Although she mixes old and new styles in her *kana* phonetic characters, she makes only one mistake in her Chinese *kanji* characters. Her handwriting is juvenile and sloppy, but she writes each letter neatly without running them together. Her sentences are very easy to understand and clearly convey her meaning. I suppose it's just because she finished elementary school, but still I think any girl from a fishing village who can write such a long and detailed letter must be rather bright.

In the middle of the letter, she mentions *namako* or "sea cucumber"; these were in fact rice cakes shaped like sea cucumber. The paper is torn just below that, rendering the next two characters illegible, but presumably she wrote that only two rice cakes were left in the package when it arrived. Demobilized soldiers also appear in the letter. This was a phenomenon of the immediate postwar era. The spring after she wrote this letter, Hatsu visited Katsuyama, to which the family had been evacuated. We must have received several other letters from her but, alas, all the rest are lost. In one, she wrote that enemy planes were frequently seen conducting raids on even her remote fishing village, and villagers ran into the mountains to hide when they approached. Raikichi still remembers seeing the word *shūyoku* in that letter, meaning "foul wings." At the time, the newspapers were using such words to refer to American bombers. But wasn't it clever of Hatsu to learn such a difficult word from the paper and use it in her letter!

That May, the Chikura household decamped from Katsuyama and moved to Kyoto. Hatsu went with them. It wasn't easy to find a suitable house, so at first they rented rooms in a house belonging to some people named Kamei, just up Imadegawa Road from the Teramachi neighborhood. An easygoing elderly lady was living on her own there. There were two rooms on the second floor divided by a corridor, and the first floor was the same. There was also a kitchen and bathroom, and a garden and so on. It was relatively comfortable, so the Chikuras rented the two rooms on the second floor. The elderly lady was kind and good-natured. "You needn't confine yourselves to the second floor," she told them. "Feel free to take your meals in the dining room. And please make use of the kitchen, too." Meanwhile, she kept to a room with a long iron brazier, shutting herself in there with Hatsu as if they were best friends. She had an adult son, but he lived apart from her in Kyoto's Nakagyō ward, for work, so perhaps she was happy to have the house full of life again. Soon after Raikichi's family moved in, Asukai Jirō, the husband of Sanko's little sister Nioko, who had been working in Hokkaido, quit his job there and came to Kyoto, where he got a job as the manager at the officers' club that had been built in the botanical gardens for the occupation forces. Before long, the two of them moved into the empty room on the first floor. With that, the Kamei house was suddenly crowded with people—six in all, with the lady of the house, Raikichi, Sanko, Mutsuko, Jirō, and Nioko, plus Hatsu.

While all this was going on, Haru, who had moved out to Amagasaki, came to visit the Kamei house with her husband, who had been repatriated from the southern islands. They said that they were hoping to find work in Kyoto. Sanko, remembering a farming family with whom she had a slight connection in a place outside the city called Ichihara, on the Kurama Electric Rail line, rented a room from them for Haru and her husband. While her husband Nakanobu was trying in vain to find work, Haru stopped by the house from time to time to see Hatsu, with whom she had always been close, and to help out in the kitchen, but before long Nakanobu was hired by a small used bookstore in Ushinomiya-chō, in Kyoto. Haru started working at the bookstore's night-stall near the Tōji temple in Kujō, eager to earn as much as possible to help her husband, so she no longer had a chance to visit the Kamei house. It must have been around this time that Hatsu sent a letter to her family back home, summoning a girl named Ume. By this time, the world was settling down little by little, and the Chikura family was getting used to their new life in Kyoto, so I think Sanko must have said, *Let's find someone to help in the kitchen*, and Hatsu must have agreed to search for a suitable girl.

Chapter Five

WHEN UME FIRST CAME TO KYOTO, SOMETHING HAP-
pened that I have never been able to forget. Ume ("Ume," or "Plum,"
was the name the Chikura family called her by; her real name was
"Kuni," that is, "Nation") was seventeen according to the old way of
reckoning, so today we would say she was fifteen or sixteen. She had
graduated from the advanced course of the same elementary school
as Hatsu and lived with her parents for a few years. When Hatsu's
letter arrived, she decided to put her hometown behind her and take
the long, long solitary trip that ended with her alighting at Kyoto
Station. Usually, when a new girl came from Kagoshima, her family
would wait until some acquaintance of theirs was making the trip
and ask that person to accompany her, but in Ume's case, unfortunately, it seemed a suitable traveling companion was not to be found,
and so the poor girl was dropped off at the platform all by herself.
Then — there must have been a telegram beforehand concerning her
arrival, and Hatsu certainly intended to go to the station to meet her,
but I suppose there was a mistake in the telegram; in any case — when

Ume got off the train at Kyoto, there was no one there to meet her. Figuring that there was nothing else for it, she picked up her heavy luggage and, since she knew the address, she set off in the direction of the Kamei house, through several neighborhoods to Imadegawa.

As you know, when I say "through several neighborhoods to Imadegawa," it means that she traveled right across Kyoto, starting from Shichijō Station on the southern edge and going all the way to the other side. This was just after the war, so of course she couldn't hail a taxi or anything like that. She caught a streetcar in front of the station and took it to Karasuma-Imadegawa and from there she wandered for three or four hours, asking the way as she walked. It was evening by the time she found the Kamei house.

"My name is Kuni," she announced, then slid open the lattice gate and entered. The Chikura family, who had been waiting anxiously, breathed a sigh of relief; at the same time, they were both shocked and impressed as they thought to themselves, *Imagine, such a pretty little girl making that trip all by herself!*

They were also impressed that this girl, unlike Hatsu, spoke standard Japanese clearly and fluently from the very start. Hatsu had never managed to lose her accent completely, and still said *kadara* instead of *karada* for "body" and *yorare* instead of *yodare* for "drool," but Ume used dialect only when speaking with Hatsu, and to Raikichi and the others she responded in clear, standard Japanese. As she wandered through the neighborhoods of Kyoto searching for the Kamei house, the fact that she had been able to stop people on the street, tell them the address, and ask the way was surely because she had this command of standard language, and not just the difficult Kagoshima dialect. Before Hatsu summoned a new girl from her hometown, cautious as she was, she would first conduct extensive inquiries, and she wouldn't proceed unless she was certain *this girl will be fine.* She was unlikely to make a mistake. This little incident demonstrated that Ume possessed just the sort of native intelligence you would expect of someone who had measured up to Hatsu's standard.

Since she was just seventeen, she was probably still growing; even so, Ume did not have as impressive a physique as Hatsu. She was a short, chubby girl with a round, pale face. Someone said she looked just like a *kokeshi* doll, and from then on everyone took to calling her that: Kokeshi doll! Kokeshi doll! I mentioned above that it was a fine custom of Kagoshima to respect one's seniors, even if they were only a year older. Well, this was especially true of Ume. She listened to all Hatsu's instructions nodding "Yes. Yes." and obeyed them absolutely. Wondering what would compel parents to send such a young girl, just out of elementary school, on such a long trip all by herself, Sanko asked Ume one day about conditions back home. Both her father and mother were dead. Her father had gotten drunk one day and set off on a bicycle, only to fall into the river, where he died. She was her parents' only daughter, but her grandfather's older sister was still in good health and kept a respectable house, and she had taken in Ume and raised her.

Just after Ume arrived, the Chikura family found a suitable house for sale in Kawaramachi, near Nanzenji temple, and moved into it. That was toward the end of 1946, in late November. It was not very far from the Eikan-dō temple, famous for its fall foliage. Outside the tatami room was a little garden, and in front of the garden, a brook, the Shirakawa, ran from north to south. Charmed by the thought of sitting at his desk in the study and listening to the murmur of the brook, Raikichi settled on the house without a second thought. If you stepped out of the front door and walked just a little way, you were at Saifukuji temple, where the great author and poet Ueda Akinari is buried. Konchi-in was nearby too, with its famous garden laid out by Kobori Enshū, and the garden of Yamagata Aritomo's villa, Murin-an. The Heian Shrine was also close.

After Raikichi and the others moved out, only Nioko and her husband Jirō remained at the Kamei house, but soon they rented a teahouse in the grounds of a villa owned by the Mitsui clan, near the Great Bridge over the Kamo River, and they moved out too.

Almost every day, after she had seen Jirō off to the officers' club in the botanical gardens, Nioko would come over to her older sister's house in Nanzenji to spend the day. It was at the end of winter the following year that Raikichi and his family, unable to bear the cold of another Kyoto winter, escaped to Atami—the place that had become so very dear to them—and stayed until spring. They no longer had the villa there, in Nishiyama, that they had abandoned during the war—they had disposed of that when they were again evacuated from Katsuyama in Okayama province—and so for the time being they rented a villa belonging to a Mr. T, in the grounds of the Atami Sannō Hotel, a branch of the famous Tokyo hotel. However, that left Mutsuko alone in the Nanzenji house, so they asked Nioko and her husband to move there and look after the house in their absence. As a result, they had to hire a few new maids: one for the villa in Atami; one to look after the Mitsui tea house while Nioko and her husband stayed at the Nanzenji house; and one more for the Nanzenji house, since there were now three people staying there, and the one maid there was no longer sufficient. Haru immediately sent for two girls from Kagoshima, called "Miki" and "Mashi."

The two girls came on the same train. Mashi had been in service at a house in the Osaka-Kobe region before returning to her hometown during the war, so this was not her first trip. "Mashi" was another unusual name. I suppose it must have been a corruption of "Masu" or "Masa," but no matter how many times Sanko asked her, she replied, "No, ma'am, it's 'Mashi.'" She claimed she had even seen it written down that way in the family register. She was about twenty-five years old, short, with a bad complexion, beady eyes, a flat nose, and indistinct features. Miki had been brought along by Mashi; it was her first time in Kansai. She was sixteen years old. She was an impatient girl who jumped to conclusions and had a habit, when being given instructions to do something, of dashing off without listening till the end. And so it was decided that, for the present, Hatsu would stay at Atami, Mashi at the Mitsui villa, and Ume and Miki at the Nanzenji house. Mashi and Miki were to be called by their real names; giving new names to servants was another practice that fell out of fashion after the war.

Raikichi and his wife stayed at Atami until the middle of April. After that, they were going back and forth all the time between Kyoto and Atami. The maids, too, were continually shifted about, with Hatsu going and Ume coming, and Miki or Mashi being sent to look after the Atami house. In addition to these four, there may have been one or two others who came for a short time and then moved on to someplace else, but they were all Kagoshima girls and acquaintances of Hatsu's. Hatsu herself had become so perfectly accustomed to Kyoto that she went out on her own every day to do the shopping at the market in Nishiki Street.

Now then, it was in the evening of the day of Setsubun, the Bean-Throwing Festival at the beginning of February, in 1948, and Raikichi and the others had left for Atami. Jirō and Nioko, Mutsuko, and Ume and Mashi were looking after the Nanzenji house. Mutsuko was sleeping on the second floor in the east-facing room, and Jirō and Nioko in the west-facing room. It must have been close to dawn, around five o'clock, when someone came dashing up the staircase and pounded on the sliding door to Mutsuko's room, crying, "Miss! Miss!"

"Who is that?!"

In Mashi's trembling voice came the reply: "Miss! Something's happened to Ume!"

"Something's happened? What do you mean?!"

"Her eyes are rolled back in her head and she's rattling the sliding screen! I'm frightened, Miss!"

Mutsuko followed Mashi downstairs. The sliding screen was rattling as if the earth were quaking. When she slid open the screen, there was Ume, her eyes rolled back, frothing at the mouth like a crab, her hands and feet trembling like a windup toy. Jirō and Nioko, alarmed, came downstairs too and found Ume, usually as pretty as a doll, glaring fiercely, her entire face contorted in bizarre fashion, her body bent backward and convulsing on her mattress. The rattling noise was the sound of the impact as she kicked at the screen and thrashed her limbs. Nioko immediately called the family doctor, a man named Kojima, still in his thirties and single, a very sociable and entertaining man, who dashed right over, took one look at Ume's condition, and said without hesitation, "Ah. It's epilepsy."

Epilepsy?! Nioko thought to herself, *that's absurd*. Ume had always been such an exceptionally bright girl. Besides, she'd been with the family for over a year now, and had never had a single seizure. Perhaps some injury had damaged Ume's brain, she thought, but Doctor Kojima disagreed: "No, this is clearly epilepsy." With that, he had the members of the household pin down the hands and feet of the patient, whose whole body was writhing and convulsing, and finally injected her with an antispasmodic drug. While he was injecting her, the sick girl struggled as she moaned something incessantly, but by and by she sprang up and then sat back down, and suddenly fell fast asleep, using Doctor Kojima's lap as her pillow. What a bizarre scene it was! Everyone was flabbergasted.

The next day, Ume was still in a stupor. The day before, Hatsu had gone to the Mitsui villa to take Mashi's place, so she was absent when the uproar began, but early the next morning she had a call from Mutsuko, and was told to trade places with Mashi again and return to the Nanzenji house immediately. The reason for this was that Mashi had been in a state of terror since seeing the expression on Ume's face the night before, with her eyes rolled back and bulging out; unable to concentrate on her work, she could only tremble all over. It was decided that, in the circumstances, Hatsu would be more reliable.

However, that too turned out to be a big mistake. By the time Hatsu returned to the house, the patient had settled down, at least for the time being, and was sleeping peacefully. Hatsu would peer into the room occasionally to gaze with evident fascination on the face of the soundly sleeping Ume. Then suddenly the patient, thinking of something, shot up and, moving like a sleepwalker, quietly slid open the screen and walked out. Mutsuko and Hatsu were astonished.

"Ume!" They called to her. "Where are you going? Are you all right?"

But she did not answer them or react in any way. Staring fixedly at a point in space, she walked soundlessly down the corridor, went to the toilet below, opened that door and gravely did her business, then soundlessly headed back out and returned to the bedroom, where she promptly fell back into a sound sleep. Walking down the corridor, her eyes were fixed, as before, on a point in the empty air before her.

The sight was so bizarre that now Hatsu began to tremble, just as she had when, years ago, the mute beggar had shown up at the house, and she had shouted "*Apa! Apa!*" her word for "mute." That evening, Hatsu laid her pillow beside Ume's and fell asleep, but as the night wore on, the trembling began again. The household was thrown into confusion, thinking that the sick girl was having a seizure, but it was not Ume thrashing about this time; it was Hatsu, plagued by nightmares and hallucinations after the dreadful afternoon. As Hatsu herself came to realize that these were hallucinations, she became even more horrified, and the trembling worsened.

Needless to say, a detailed account of this incident arrived almost immediately at the house in Atami, where Raikichi and his wife were staying. Nioko's husband, Asukai Jirō, was a man of many talents, and he was particularly good at drawing cartoons, so he had illustrated the letter with a detailed drawing of Ume thrashing about, her hair tangled like a briar patch. And yet, Raikichi and his wife wondered, why had such an intelligent girl, the sort who brilliantly performed any task you asked of her, been cursed with such a disease? Could they be absolutely certain that it was epilepsy, as Doctor Kojima had said? They wanted to do whatever could be done to cure her and decided that, upon returning to Kyoto, they would take her to see a specialist at Kyoto University or Osaka University. Happily, in February, the seizures ceased for a few days, and Ume was back to her old self, but as February turned to March they received notice that the seizures had begun again, continuing for two or three days at a time. Nioko wrote in a letter that, while she couldn't be sure if it was the cause of the seizures or not, Ume had gone to get her first permanent wave two or three days before they started. What's more, it hadn't been her own idea to get a perm; Haru, the girl whose husband, Nakanobu, worked at the used bookstore, had insisted that a perm would be a good idea. Now, in those days, there was no such thing as a cold perm, only the hot kind. The customer was subjected to quite a bit of heat and just had to put up with it. Afterward, Ume said that she had barely been able to stand the heat on her head. Wasn't it likely, Nioko wrote, that the seizures had been provoked by that stimulus?

Chapter Six

SANKO TOOK UME TO BE DIAGNOSED IN THE NEU-
rology Department at Osaka University Hospital in mid-April. Having viewed the cherry blossoms at Nishikigaura in Atami, husband and wife had returned to Kyoto and, after first visiting the Heian Shrine to see the famous double weeping cherry trees in bloom, she took Ume to Osaka the following day. The conclusion was that Ume undoubtedly suffered from epilepsy, just as Doctor Kojima had said. Asked by the doctor, "Do you remember ever falling from a high place and hitting your head hard when you were a child?" Ume had responded, "Now that you mention it, Doctor, when I was about four, I fell from the roof and hit my head."

"That was the cause, then. Ordinarily, seizures begin in puberty, but in your case, you went this long without incident until by chance the heat from the permanent wave acted as a stimulus, and the seizures began. Now, hereditary epilepsy is quite difficult to cure, but yours is acquired, so there's no cause for pessimism. If you continue taking your daily dose of an antispasmodic called phenytoin, then the seizures will become less and less severe until they eventually cease. The very best treatment, however, is marriage. If you'll just get married, your recovery is guaranteed," so the specialist informed them.

Despite this, Ume's condition did not improve as easily as that Osaka University specialist had said. One or two years later, she returned to her hometown and married Hatsu's older brother, and she now has two children, a boy and a girl. No trace of her epilepsy remains, so the doctor's prognosis was correct in the end, but she continued to suffer from occasional seizures while she was working in the Chikura household, shocking and distressing the others.

In April of 1949, the Chikura household turned the Nanzenji house over to Nioko and her husband and moved to a house near the sacred grove called Tadasu no Mori, or "the Forest of Correction," in the Shimogamo Shrine. The new house had many rooms, and so again it was necessary to hire additional maids. The two that were hired, Koma and Sada, came not through Hatsu but at the recommendation of a kimono-maker who often came to the house. Koma was a Kyoto native, and Sada was from Kawachi, in Osaka. I'll have an opportunity to discuss their backgrounds and natures later on, so I won't go into detail now. Before we get to all that: soon after arriving, these two observed the spectacle of Ume rattling the screen doors, and they reacted in very different ways.

Koma, who joined the household one or two months before Sada, had one strange habit. If anything made her feel at all uncomfortable, she would immediately get the dry heaves. These were accompanied by a great deal of loud moaning. Even very minor things would cause this—seeing a spider in the hall, or a centipede falling from the ceiling. Sometimes, as she began to heave, she would panic and fly out of the house, and at such times, the heaves continued until she actually threw up. Whenever Ume had a seizure and started to rattle the doors of the maids' room, Koma began to heave and ran out of the room, holding her mouth. It only exacerbated the uproar. And it got even worse once Sada joined the household, for she would begin quivering with fear and then run out, crying "Mother!"

Sanko took Ume to Osaka University Hospital once more to have her examined. The attacks generally occurred once a month, just before or after menstruation, and Ume would have a sort of premonition a few days before.

"I feel strange. There's somehow—," she would say.

The expression "There's somehow—" was peculiar to Kagoshima. Hatsu, Etsu, Miki, and Mashi; they all used it to mean "Something's wrong." According to Ume, starting several days before an attack, her head was filled to overflowing with bizarrely complicated and mysterious visions, and she was overcome by an indescribably unpleasant feeling. Not just one vision, but two or three at the same time and completely unrelated would enter into her head. Various thoughts, separate and unconnected, would arise in her mind and develop in disjointed fashion. The experience was so eerie that she could hardly stand it. As the time drew near, others, too, would recognize, "Ume's about to have another attack." Sometimes she would chase around after Koma or Sada, cackling and tickling their backside or armpits; that was a sign that the attacks were about to begin. She only chased after women, though; never men.

The severity of her condition varied somewhat in those days from month to month, but without fail, when the seizures came, Ume would lose control of her bladder. And when they subsided, she would fall asleep, snoring loudly. Once, when the seizures began, she stood up casually, climbed onto the kitchen drain-board, and, lifting one leg like a dog, relieved herself. If she experienced any sort of nervous excitement or shock, she could have an attack even though it was not her time of the month.

During 1949, once again, the Chikura household maintained two residences, the main house and a villa. The main house was the one near the Forest of Correction, and the villa was one they had taken in a part of Atami called Nakada, after moving out of the other on the grounds of the Sannō Hotel, which they had rented from a Mr. T. As a result, the number of maids in Kyoto and Atami increased once again. When Raikichi and his wife were in Atami on New Year's Eve, wintering there as usual, Ume and Koma stayed with them, and there must have been one more maid, but I'm not sure who that was. Anyway, leaving that third maid aside, after they had finished preparing the special New Year's foods, Ume and Koma got permission from their master to go into town and watch a movie. It was at a theater run by Tōhō, and the movie was something called *Waterloo Bridge,* starring Robert Taylor and Vivien Leigh. The theater was almost empty on New Year's Eve. Before long, Koma began to cry and talk back to the movie screen in a voice overflowing with emotion. Ume, sitting next to her, was aghast:

"Koma! What are you doing, speaking in such a loud voice? Everyone is staring at us!"

Again and again she scolded and prodded her, but Koma wouldn't stop. Sometimes the sound of her dry heaves was mixed in. Each time that happened, the people in surrounding seats turned to stare. Finally, unable to put up with it any longer, Ume changed her seat, moving to the opposite side of the theater, as far as possible from Koma. Even at that distance, though, she could clearly hear Koma's sobs, and at first she watched the movie shaking in anger. Somehow, though, Koma's sobs were contagious, and soon Ume felt an unbearable sadness well up within her and, with a sudden, loud sob, she began crying too. And so, the two girls' noisy sobs rang through the theater until the end of the movie. The seizure that struck Ume early the next morning, on the first day of 1950, was no doubt a result of that evening's emotional outburst, and it was more severe than usual.

The Great Atami Fire occurred in mid-April of that year, beginning on the evening of the thirteenth and continuing until dawn. Raikichi and the others were in Kyoto at the time, having left the Nakada house in the care of Ume and another maid, called Sayo. The fire, which had begun on reclaimed land at the shore, gradually spread along one side toward the mountains. Raikichi and the others in Kyoto heard reports over the radio that the flames were drawing nearer to the Nakada house moment by moment, and at one point they had completely given up any hope of the villa being saved, but dawn brought the good news that the fire had spared it, if just barely. Throughout that night, Ume and Sayo had performed an extraordinary feat, packing any household items they thought valuable into trunks, bags, and cloth bundles and moving them to the home of an acquaintance in Nishiyama, climbing that steep mountain road I don't know how many times. Raikichi and his wife returned to Atami from Kyoto while the embers were still smoldering to find the town's fashionable spots reduced to ashes all about them. First they wanted to thank the maids for their efforts. As they entered the front door, they called out, "Thank you so much for all your hard work last night. It must have been terrible for you both."

Then Sayo came out by herself to greet them. "How fortunate that the house escaped harm! Sensei's luck is very strong." She was the kind of woman to speak in this strangely impertinent manner even under such conditions.

"And Ume? Where is she?"

Sayo looked troubled. "Ume is on the second-floor balcony."

"On the balcony?"

Just as they began to climb the stairway to the second floor, the sound of a tremendous snore drifted down to them. When they got to the second floor and had a look, they found Ume fast asleep, faceup on the sun-drenched balcony. Beside her ran a little trail of urine. When they questioned Sayo, she told them that Ume had labored by her side the night before, but that perhaps the power of the blazing fire had overstimulated her, for around noon the next day, Ume had gone out to the balcony to stare at the charred landscape and, as she did, her behavior had grown stranger until at last the usual seizure had struck and she began thrashing around. Until now, Ume's seizures had always occurred in the evening, never during the day, but this time, they occurred at midday. Then she had collapsed from exhaustion right where she was.

I wrote that Ume would return to normal once a seizure had ended, but according to Koma, when she lay down to sleep next to Ume in the evening, Ume tried to wrap her legs around Koma's. Also, Ume liked to drink, and sometimes, in the kitchen, she finished off the leftover *sake* that had gone cold after dinner. One time, in Kyoto, she had been permitted a drink in public, and got so terribly drunk that she grabbed Mutsuko's older brother Keisuke and shouted at him, "Hey! Bring me some water!"

When she was required to cook, Ume was rather skilled, thanks to Hatsu's training. She was best at omelets. First, she would spread the eggs to a thin, even layer in the frying pan, and then she would top this with ham, ground meat, *nori,* or fish, and wrap the egg around it. Next, shouting "Hey! Hey! Hey!" she would toss the omelet in the air and flip it over. Koma called this the "swallow roll." She often called to the others, "Look! Ume's about to do her swallow roll!"

Ume's actions were slow but surprisingly deft. One thing about her that was different from most people was the way she held the knife when peeling daikon radish or potatoes. Most people, when they grip the knife handle, wrap their four fingers around the side opposite the thumb, but Ume would lay her index finger along the ridge of the knife blade, leaving the three other fingers wrapped around the handle and, like this, could peel vegetables expertly, the skins falling away in coils. It wasn't just Ume; Hatsu, Etsu, Miki, and Mashi, and Sada and Gin, who will appear later—all the Kagoshima girls peeled vegetables this way.

Ume also had a sense of humor, and got Sanko's jokes more quickly than anyone else. Apparently, in Kagoshima, when they should say "*Tayasui koto de gozaimasu*" or "That's easy," people just say "*Yasui koto de gozaimasu,*" which sounds the same as "That's cheap," so when Ume was asked once, "Could you do this?" instead of "No problem," she seemed to respond "That's cheap!" Raikichi heard about this before long and, in response to something, he mimicked Ume, saying "That's cheap!" So the next time, Ume turned the tables, mimicking Raikichi's voice as she said "That's cheap," and made everyone laugh.

It was in the year after the Great Fire that Ume requested leave to return to her hometown. At that time, the seizures were occurring once a month, and it wasn't unusual for her to sleep through the next day without eating a thing. Three or four years after that, when the Chikura household received word that she had married Hatsu's brother Yasukichi, who had been earning his living on a fishing boat ever since he was a boy, they were as happy as could be, and relieved too, and they all toasted her happiness. When Sanko heard that Ume had a new baby girl, it was exactly one year after Mutsuko's brother Keisuke, here, had married and had a girl, so she was constantly sending Ume all sorts of baby clothes and other things that were no longer needed, and each time she received an acknowledgement, saying that, thanks to her generosity, they had not needed to make any clothes for the baby. In this way, letters continued back and forth between them, and Ume sometimes sent them half-dried bonito and other such treats, but they had no chance to learn what sort of a wife she had become or even what she looked like after eleven years—until very recently. Sometimes, though, her husband, Yasukichi, who had been promoted to chief engineer of the bonito fishing boat, would happen to drop anchor at the famous fishing port of Yaizu in Shizuoka while out on an expedition. On those occasions he would always stop by Atami for a visit, bringing an enormous bonito as a gift, and they'd get caught up on news of his wife and children. Looking into his face, Raikichi and the others thought not only of Ume, but of his sister Hatsu, whom he resembled, as well. They looked forward to his visit each year as the season for bonito approached, wondering if he would come again. As the years went by, though, his visits gradually became less frequent. The fishing boats were probably venturing out beyond the Japan Sea coast more frequently, to the China Sea and the Indian Ocean.

The fishing boats from their area were wooden, with diesel engines, one hundred and fifty tons at most and as small as thirty tons. The boat Yasukichi worked on was about fifty tons; even so, its main purpose was deep-sea fishing. He told them that they caught the bonito with fishing poles, using small, live fish as bait. There were about fifty crew members. In addition to the ship's captain and the head of fishing operations, there were a chief engineer, radio communication operators, navigation officers, spotters, helmsmen, rudder operators, and so on. The ship carried fuel oil; water for holding the live fish bait, which were mackerel and sardines; food supplies and drinking water; and a full complement of fishing rods and tackle. The bonito ride the Kuroshio Current, swimming north at the beginning of spring and south in late autumn. They are nimble by nature, and generally travel in schools. They eat plankton in addition to small fish. The ship operated mainly from the area around the Tokara Islands to the islands southwest of Okinawa and the coastal waters off Taiwan. Each fishing trip lasted one to three weeks, but they operated year-round with almost no break, so the men could go back home and see their wives and children for only a day or two a month.

Chapter Seven

THERE MUST BE A LOT OF INTERESTING AND UN-
usual stories on a fishing boat—won't you tell us some?" Raikichi
entreated Yasukichi when he came to visit a few years ago.

"Oh yes, there are. I could tell you some strange stories, if Sir and
Madam care to listen. I'm not well educated and I'm not much of a
storyteller, but if I can get a friend to write them down for me, I'll
send them to you," Yasukichi replied. "I hope you'll enjoy them."
Sure enough, a letter arrived just one month later with the following manuscript enclosed. It had been written down by a friend of
Yasukichi's, apparently a man of considerable ability, who had once
worked on the same ship as Yasukichi and was now a clerk at a town
hall somewhere. Please read it, therefore, not as a mere transcription
of Yasukichi's words, but also as that writer's composition. It's a bit
long, but I think it will help you understand Hatsu, Ume, and others
such as Setsu who came after them. Let me start by transcribing part
of the opening section:

Tomari Harbor at dawn is still silent. In the dark of the nearby shore, cheerful voices call to one another. Suddenly, the sound of a lively popular song fills the harbor, playing over a speaker on the ship, a bonito-fishing boat moored in the harbor. After returning to port yesterday with a big catch, the ship is setting out again. The sky finally begins to brighten in the east, and fishermen crowded onto a small barge row out from the wharf to the ship. A flag flying from the ship, signaling the big catch, snaps in the wind. Eventually, the ship raises anchor, starts its engines, and gently turns its prow toward the mouth of the harbor. The families and friends of the men on board are lined up along the shore, warmly waving them goodbye. The music over the loudspeaker has changed to a stirring military march, and the ship, breaking through the waves in the harbor, begins its advance into the open sea.

They have set a course for fishing grounds in the rough southern seas where the Kuroshio Current surges. They carry no bait en route. They use only the small sardines and mackerel that bonito love, and there are supplies of such bait in a village near the fishing grounds, where they stop to fill the ship's live-boxes. Once that's done, it's time to head for the fishing grounds. The southern seas of the subtropics bear the heat of perpetual summer. The crew are all naked but for their underpants and a cloth wrapped around their head, a full complement of fine young men, their skin as red as copper. The ship gets past the turbulence of the South China Sea and continues due south. There is nothing around but the deep blue sea and the sky.

From the captain on down, each man on the ship scans the horizon in every direction for a school of bonito. Wherever there is a school of fish, sea birds swarm and circle above. These birds are gannets, which the men call the "bonito bird." Spotting them on the far-off horizon is a grave responsibility in the fishing grounds. Standing on the bridge, under the blazing sun, the men never take their eyes from their binoculars; the spotters take turns climbing up to the watch tower on the mast and diligently scanning the sea. All day long, the ship circles the boundless ocean, searching.

The radio communications operator in the telegraph room maintains contact with stations along the coast, picking up the meteorological observatory's weather reports to help ensure the ship's safe voyage, as well as ascertaining the size of other ships' catches and reporting this to the head of fishing operations. The chief engineer supports the rudder operator on duty without letting his attention stray from the engine for even a moment. The captain cooperates with the head of fishing operations, constantly consulting the navigation charts to confirm the ship's position. The duties of the high-ranking crew are arduous: checking the temperature of the water, examining the condition of the live bait. What's more, there are days when they meet with not a single school of fish, and all their hard work is in vain.

Today, just before dawn, the whole crew hopped out of bed, ran from their cabins, and took their positions: another day beginning just like the last. There was a pleasant lull, and the weather was fair—a perfect day for fishing. Then, from the spotter on the mast came a shout that he spied gannets. In the engine room came the signal for full speed ahead. The ship turned to the southwest and then sped forward, straight as an arrow. The fishermen set up their rods in a line. Like a hound chasing down its quarry, the ship rushes to where the bonito birds flock at the water's surface. As the men responsible for scattering bait hurl it energetically into the sea, the bonito surge to the surface, as if they would leap from the water. The veteran hands begin the first round of fishing. The boat cuts its engine and comes to a stop. The other men scatter bait over the sea unsparingly. From the great school of bonito one fish takes the bait and is flipped up onto the deck of the ship. All at once the deck of the ship is like a battlefield, seething with bloodlust, as dozens of bamboo fishing rods spring up and one man after another begins to cast. Sprayers hang from the sides of the ship, and water pours down like a rainstorm onto the bonito at the surface, confusing them.

The ship's boys run here and there across the deck, bringing the fishermen buckets of bait. The caught fish raise a din as they're tossed aside, flapping their chests and tailfins against the deck. The silver of their bellies glitters beautifully. In the blink of an eye, a mountain of fish piles up, till there's no place to stand. From a crowd of fish so great that it seemed to change the color of the sea, thousands have been caught, beyond counting. The ship lies low in the water with the weight of them. It can't hold any more. The captain's command, "Stop fishing!" resounds in a loud voice. The fishermen breathe a sigh of relief.

The tanks that held the live bait are quickly converted to storage for the bonito. The valves for letting sea water in and out of the live-tanks are shut and the water is pumped out, then they are filled with ice to keep the fish fresh as the ship returns to its base, the fish market. The ship's progress is slow, but every member of the crew wears a cheerful expression. How many days has it been since they left home port? As the ship was sailing through stormy waters, they often said, "One step below these planks is Hell"; during that time, their one dream, morning and night, was today's big catch. Here and there on deck, boastful tales of their exploits spring up.

At last, they've arrived back at their home port. The flag signaling a big catch flashes from the main mast. A siren rings out within the harbor. Lined up along the deck, the crew altogether rousingly shout the call for a big catch: "Han yo—i yo—i hanyoi saa saa!"

This diary was written to emphasize as much as possible the heroic aspects of the job, but it's not difficult to imagine how hard life was for the wives of the crewmen on these ships. Having married Hatsu's brother Yasukichi, Ume was happy to have recovered from her terrible illness and borne two children, but it was not the sort of life where you welcome your husband home from work each day and sit down to supper together with him and the children. She could do that only once or twice a month. She spent most of the year in loneliness, a baby in each arm, worrying about Yasukichi. The manuscript includes the line, "One step below these planks is Hell." Her husband sets out on a fifty-ton diesel ship to seek out fishing grounds as far away as the South China Sea and no sooner has he returned home for a rare visit than he's back on the ship the next morning, heading out of the harbor. Every time she saw him off, as she steeled herself against the pain welling up within, Ume must have thought, "Could this be the last time I see my husband's face?" Even if he came home only once or twice a month, that was fine, so long as he did come home, but one day he might go off and never return. In recent years, weather forecasts have become more reliable, and sea voyages are safer, but at the time that Ume married, shipwrecks were by no means unusual: another maid who joined the household later, Setsu—her first husband crewed with a bonito ship, too, and one day, not two years after they married, he went out on a fishing trip and never came back.

When this Setsu came into service with the Chikura household, she had already lost her husband and was a young widow of just twenty-four with a three-year-old son. She had chosen to leave her hometown and her cute little boy behind—even though that wasn't absolutely necessary. The fact was that the boy was not at all attached to her; when her husband was alive and off working on the bonito ship, she'd leave their son with her mother-in-law and go to work in the fields, and the boy had become more like his grandmother's child. Kagoshima held nothing but sad memories for her, Setsu said, and was a dull place with no fun at all to be had, so she had gone into service. Now, I hear, she's happily married to a master mechanic in a certain factory in Kita-Kyushu. I'm sure she'd had enough of being a fisherman's wife. Then again, there are plenty of instances of widows in that neighborhood who married another fisherman only to have the second husband die too. In a fishing village where land is scarce and other real jobs are hard to come by, one has little choice but to marry a fisherman. Why, only very recently, Raikichi received word that Ume's husband, Yasukichi, had finally left his ship and come to Kobe and found some other work (though he didn't say what sort exactly). Thankfully, he never met with any great misfortune, but he must have grown anxious, thinking of the future of his wife and children.

And now we come to Setsu's story, but first I have to tell you about Sayo, with whom Setsu had a close connection.

When the Great Fire struck in April of 1950, Sayo was the caretaker at the house the family had rented in the Nakada neighborhood of Atami. It was she who, covered in ash — together with Ume — had done such a tremendous job and then, the next day, had witnessed the spectacle of Ume's severe seizure, so she must have come to live in the Chikura household in March of that year. She was not one of those girls who came to us thanks to Hatsu — not a member of the "Kagoshima Prefectural Association." Koma, from Kyoto, and Sada, from Kawachi, both came through the assistance of the kimono-maker, but Sayo had no recommendation at all; she simply came to Sanko one day and offered her services, saying, "Excuse me, ma'am, could you use me in your household?"

When the Chikuras were living below Nanzenji on Kawaramachi Avenue, Sayo was working for a man named Nakamura, the president of a certain bank, who had a mansion not far away in Eikandō-cho. Every day, on her master's instructions, she went out to buy groceries and, passing the front gate of the Chikura house on her way back and forth, she became friendly with Sanko and the maids and got into the habit of stepping through the back door into the kitchen to chat for a while. In retrospect, it does seem that she already had some ulterior motive to probe the intimate recesses of the Chikura house, but the clueless Chikuras simply thought to themselves, "She looks like she'll do fine," and hired her without asking for references or proof of identity or anything like that. As a result, it was somewhat unclear whether she had asked Mr. Nakamura to let her go or had been fired. She looked to be around thirty, give or take, and it seemed she had been in service someplace else before the Nakamura house, but we knew nothing for certain. Sanko engaged her services when the household moved from Nanzenji to the area near the Shimogamo Shrine and, at that time, she did go once to the Nakamura house to get a reference for Sayo, but, unfortunately, neither the master of the house nor its mistress were at home, and so she went ahead and engaged Sayo on faith.

According to what Sanko learned indirectly from Koma, Sayo was from Awa, or Tokushima as it's now called, on the island of Shikoku, and she did mention certain things—for example, "My mother brought me with her to her second marriage"—but she seemed not to want to talk about her past, so we didn't ask her for more details. Her work habits when she joined the Chikura household were or- dinary—there was no problem you could point to—only, Raikichi, for no particular reason, took an immediate dislike to her.

"That maid that just started, Sayo—I don't suppose you could let her go?"

"But why?"

"I can't really say why … call it intuition; she makes me uncom- fortable. I just can't stand that girl."

"But she just started. It really wouldn't do to dismiss her without any reason. And she worked so hard during the Great Fire."

This conversation between husband and wife occurred while they were staying at the Nakada house, after going to offer their condolences to victims of the fire, and it must have been an evening then toward the end of May when Raikichi, reading in the study on the second floor, happened to open the desk drawer and discov- ered inside a neatly folded piece of paper that he did not recognize. Wondering what it could be, he unfolded it and found the following message hastily written in pencil:

"I found myself in need of a pencil and so I have borrowed one from here. Please forgive my presumption. Sayo."

The handwriting and the style of expression were perfectly proper and not unskillful. But when had Sayo placed the paper in the desk drawer? Raikichi opened the drawer two or three times a day. He had opened it once that morning, and again around two or three in the afternoon, but he didn't recall seeing the paper in there then. After that, he'd gone downstairs to the parlor after three and had a snack, then stepped out to the garden and tended the potted plants for a little while, and then read the evening paper until, around five thirty, he went back upstairs to the study. Sometime during that span of barely two hours, she must have seen her chance and tossed the note in the drawer. There were at least ten pencils on the pen tray; if she'd needed one, she could simply have taken one of these. No—there was no need to do even that. She could have gone to the maids' room, where Ume or Koma or someone else was bound to have a pencil.

Flushed with anger, Raikichi shouted, "Hello? Sayo! Is Sayo here? Please come upstairs!"

Chapter Eight

IS SAYO HERE? SAYO!"

"You summoned me, Sir?" Weirdly calm and excessively polite, as usual, Sayo had climbed the stairs without a sound, softly slid open the door, and knelt down.

"It was you, wasn't it, who opened this drawer, then wrote this and put it inside?"

"I was afraid it was improper of me to have taken the liberty of borrowing a pencil—"

"I'm not talking about borrowing a pencil! I'm talking about opening your master's desk drawer! Who gave you permission to open it? It's ill-mannered to go opening people's drawers!"

"I beg your pardon, Sir. I had to write down a memo quickly, before I forgot, and so—"

"That's not what I'm asking. I'm asking who gave you permission to open this desk!"

"Yes, sir."

"There are pencils on top of the desk. There was no reason to open the drawer when you could have used one of those."

"Yes, sir."

"You bitch. You really are a strange one!" Without thinking, he let the word "bitch" slip out. "You see me every day. If you thought it was wrong to borrow the pencil, you could have apologized in person when we met. There was no need to write a note like this and leave it in the drawer."

"Yes, sir."

Raikichi was as annoyed as if she had written him a love letter.

"First of all, these pencils here are for my use when I work at this desk every day. I sharpen these pencils myself every day and arrange them in here, like this. I find it unlikely that you didn't know whether or not it was right for you to use one."

"Yes, sir."

"Idiot! Insolent girl! I don't want you here—get out!" Short-tempered by nature, Raikichi had a tendency to yell at the maids, but he had never used such severe language. He was angered right down to his core. He called for Sanko immediately and told her to dismiss Sayo. When he got upset like this, Sanko could usually soothe her husband and calm things down, but not this time.

"Of course I'm angry! I would be crazy not to be angry!"

"Well, that's true. But …" She tried saying this and that to pacify him but, as was his habit at such times, Raikichi was only further upset by her failure to share his anger.

"We don't need to give her a reason—she should know the reason! Tell her, 'My husband hates you; get out!' It disgusts me just to see her face."

"Well then, I guess it can't be helped. I'll tell her just that and ask her to leave."

"She must be a little strange in the head, don't you think?"

"Mm. As you describe her behavior, it's rather strange."

"The more I scold her, the more weirdly impassive she becomes, and the smarmier and more simpering her manner of speaking—of course I get even more annoyed. I wonder if she's losing her mind; I have a feeling she's headed that way."

In the end, at Raikichi's insistence, Sayo hurriedly packed her bags that evening and went off somewhere first thing the next morning, disappearing.

Raikichi immediately felt much better, relieved of his anxiety. As for where Sayo had disappeared to, he could imagine that Sanko had made some arrangement for her while keeping it a secret from him but, for the time being, he decided not to worry about it. Meanwhile, they sent for a girl from the Kyoto house to take Sayo's place. This was Setsu.

Setsu was one of the girls who came from Tomari, in Kagoshima, at Hatsu's recommendation. She joined the household near Shimogamo Shrine around the same time as Sayo—maybe three or four days later. She was a widow and, as I said, she had left her three-year-old child in the care of her mother-in-law. She said she was twenty-four. At first glance, she wasn't beautiful but had average looks. She and Sayo didn't live together under the same roof at the Shimogamo house for very long. They were together in March, but Sayo went to look after the Nakada house at the beginning of April, and they were parted. Then Setsu was summoned after Sayo was driven away.

"What did Sayo do after leaving us?" Raikichi, a bit uneasy, eventually asked Sanko. "Please tell me she didn't return to the Shimogamo house!"

"Sayo is in Tokyo."

"Really? Where in Tokyo?"

"A friend of mine named Harada—her maiden name was Tanabe—you remember her, don't you?"

"Oh, is Sayo working for her?"

"No, not for her. On her recommendation, she's working as a live-in maid for a friend of Harada's called Mrs. Gamō."

According to Sanko, when she dismissed her, Sayo had said, "Even if I return to Kyoto, there's no one there I can rely on … I'm all alone in this world, without a place to call home … starting tonight, I'll have no option but to sleep under a bridge or something," and Sanko hadn't known how to proceed; she couldn't leave things like that. With maids in such short supply, she thought, every household was looking for help, so surely Sayo could find a position somewhere, and then Mrs. Harada had come to mind. Of course! Harada was an obliging sort and well connected; she would find something for Sayo. "I have this maid at my house, but my husband doesn't get along with her, and told me to get rid of her immediately, and I don't know what to do," she had said. "It's not like she has any particular fault worth mentioning. She has a few eccentricities, but she works hard; in the recent fire, for example, she did all she could to move our things to safety. We were really quite grateful." And with that, Harada had responded, "Send her to me, I'll take care of her. A job will turn up before long, and in the meantime she can stay with me for a few days." Sanko had sent Sayo off to Mrs. Harada in Aoyama that morning. The timing was perfect, because Mrs. Harada found Sayo a position immediately, and so without burdening her for even one day Sayo went into service with Mrs. Harada's acquaintance Mrs. Gamō, in Ōmori.

Raikichi was reasonably intimate with his wife's old schoolmate, Mrs. Harada, but he had no dealings at all with the Gamō household, so he knew nothing in particular about them. The husband, who worked in import and export, was staying in America and would not be returning home for the next year or two, and the wife was living in the Ōmori house and looking after two school-aged children—this according to Sanko, who was merely repeating what she had heard from Mrs. Harada. After that, they heard not a word about how Sayo had worked out, nor did they think to ask. Then one day Raikichi happened to meet Mrs. Harada on a train.

"Now that I think of it, there's something I've been meaning to tell you," Mrs. Harada said, taking the seat next to Raikichi's and bringing her mouth close to his ear. "Well, you remember that maid from some time back? Her name was Sayo or something…"

"Yes, yes, what about her?"

"I have a feeling there was a perfectly good reason why you came to hate her."

"Did she do something strange again?"

"She hasn't done anything improper, exactly, since she went to the Gamō's, but…"

"Yes?"

"When was it? I spoke with your wife, and then I brought the girl to Mrs. Gamō's house, didn't I. At that time, I took the subway with her from Aoyama to Shinbashi, and then we went by train to Ōmori. It was on that train."

"I see."

"That was my first conversation with her—I had just met her for the first time. And yet, she came over and leaned into me in an over-familiar way, and whispered to me in a low voice, 'Madam, do you happen to know this poem?' Then she recited a poem in classical Japanese smoothly in one breath: 'How hard it would be to see my mother and father in such a world; they passed in good time.'"

"Hmm."

"Well now, I told her, no, I don't know that poem, so I couldn't say whose it was, and she said, 'This is Master Raikichi's poem,' and re-cited it again, modulating her voice a little: 'How hard it would be to see my mother and father in such a world; they passed in good time.'"

Sure enough, Raikichi thought, he had composed that poem; there was no doubt about it. But it had been four or five years ago, during the war. An amateur at poetry, Raikichi had never published it. Possibly it had been included, of necessity, in a literary miscellany of wartime writings, but when would Sayo have read such a thing? Raikichi found it strange.

"She knew that poem?"

"And all sorts of other things about you, besides. And she's read and heard all kinds of cheap gossip. 'I'm Sensei's biggest fan,' she said. 'I've always admired him. How many years has it been since he married that woman?' she said, and, 'I wonder if her younger sister, Miss Nioko, is satisfied in her marriage,' 'Miss Mutsuko is Madam's daughter by a previous marriage, isn't she?' and so on. She seemed to have a great interest in your family's affairs, and she kept trying to get information out of me. I soon put a stop to the conversation and refused to be drawn in, but I could see why you took such a dislike to her."

"Hm! She really said all that? When she was with us, her behavior wasn't so extreme, but it was evident that she had such tendencies. I can just imagine her talking to you that way. I hope she won't bother you again."

Raikichi parted with Mrs. Harada after this conversation and heard no more rumors about Sayo, who seemed, fortunately, to be working without incident at Ōmori.

Then, in late July, Raikichi and his wife were staying for ten days at a hotel in Hakone. They were having dinner in the hotel restaurant when a call came for them from Atami, so Sanko went to take it.

"What a nuisance!" she said as she returned to the table. "Setsu has up and quit."

"What? Is that what she said?"

"She said her mother back home is sick, so would we please let her go, it's urgent …"

"Was it Setsu you spoke to?"

"It was Ume on the phone. By 'mother,' she must mean her mother-in-law, who's looking after her child. If she's sick, she can't look after the child, I suppose, so it seems Setsu has to go home immediately. Even so, I wish she'd wait until we return. I told her we could change our plans and return two or three days earlier than planned, but she said she was too worried to wait, so would we please allow her to go back this evening by the night train."

"Couldn't she have taken the phone to tell you herself?"

"Perhaps she found it difficult to make such a presumptuous demand herself."

Raikichi had detested Sayo, but he liked Setsu, somehow; he couldn't say why, exactly. When she was made to write something down, her penmanship was skillful. He had been moved to admiration, first of all, by how her writing displayed an intellectual flair you wouldn't expect from a girl raised in the countryside with only an elementary-school education. Of course, he had never exchanged letters with her, but he'd seen envelopes she had addressed, and discarded notes written on scraps of paper, and had occasionally been surprised that the girl could write so cleverly. He'd been completely charmed. If she can write this well, he thought, she must have an excellent mind. And so, though he had never thought her a beauty, he even came to see her features as lively and quite intelligent.

"Well, if she says it's urgent, we should give her this month's wages, and I'd at least like to send her off with the price of her ticket, in lieu of a farewell gift …"

"That's what I told her, but she said it's selfish of her to return home like this, so she couldn't possibly let us pay for her ticket, and if we would be kind enough to send her this month's wages afterward, that would be fine."

"Oh really? Well then, there's nothing else to be done. Let's hope that her mother recovers, and she can come back to us—Wait. I'll call her myself and at least say goodbye." Concerned, Raikichi asked Setsu over the phone what train she was taking, what her mother's condition was, whether she would bring all her belongings home with her or have them sent by rail, and so on, but Setsu was strangely vague in her replies, not at all like her usual brisk manner of speech, but mumbling and faltering in a quiet voice, holding the phone far from her mouth, as though she were trying to get away.

"That was strange—Setsu wasn't her usual self, and I could hardly catch what she was saying."

"She's probably at loose ends, upset over her mother's illness," Sanko said.

The next morning, just to check, Sanko called Ume and asked, "Did Setsu get off all right last night?" and Ume hesitated a moment before responding.

"Madam, I don't know how to tell you this. Well ... Setsu did leave last night, but she wasn't headed for Kagoshima. She was headed for Tokyo."

Chapter Nine

WHERE IN TOKYO?"

"I'm not sure where exactly, but I think she must have gone to Sayo-san's."

"Sayo's?!"

Raikichi then interrogated her until at last, reluctantly, Ume explained. He and Sanko left Hakone and headed back to Atami that same day. According to Ume, Setsu and Sayo apparently hit it off and had become very close friends. One wouldn't have supposed it, considering how little time they spent together in the house near the Shimogamo shrine, but they'd exchanged letters constantly after they were separated, one in Kyoto and the other in Atami, and when Setsu was summoned to the Atami house to replace Sayo after she was ejected, she was constantly expressing sympathy for "poor Sayo." It was one thing to pity Sayo, but out of an excess of compassion she had gone so far as to criticize Raikichi's behavior as cruel: "Wasn't it outrageous to toss her out just because he took a dislike to her, when there was no specific problem he could point to?" she would say. "Sayo is a good person. She's honest and considerate." She'd say: "I don't think there's anyone else so nice. It's Sensei who's acting unreasonable and obstinate," and so on. "I'll say it right to his face, I will! I'll tell him straight out, 'Sensei, adjust your attitude!' As a novelist, he of all people should understand." Going on and on in this extreme way, the usually reserved Setsu sounded like a different person, Ume said.

"Really! Setsu said all that?"

"She only worked herself up to that pitch when she was defending Sayo."

Even so, Raikichi couldn't imagine Setsu's expression as she said such things.

"Ah," Sanko said, "Sayo must have instigated this whole thing, drawing Setsu toward her like a moth to flame."

"That's it. I'm sure that's it," a resentful Raikichi agreed, annoyed.

After that, Raikichi and Sanko heard nothing more of Setsu, but four or five days later, the following remarkable letter arrived for Ume.

> Please forgive me for the inconvenience I caused you the other evening. It seems they can use me in the Gamō household, so I've decided to stay here. I love Sayo so, I can barely stand it, and I'm glad that we can live together in the same house. For me, there is no greater joy than this. I hope this joy will last forever and ever.
>
> I'm sorry to trouble you, but could you forward my things, any mail, etc., to the Gamōs' address?

Sayo had completely taken in Raikichi and Sanko and, on top of that, had convinced Setsu to run off with her. It was a well-planned revenge, but that wasn't the end of the incident; there was more to come. "For me, there is no greater joy than this," Setsu had written. "I hope this joy will last forever and ever." But that hope was not to be realized. Two or three months later, there was a phone call from Mrs. Harada.

"It seems those two had an unspeakable connection," she announced in a shocked tone.

"An unspeakable connection?"

"They're lesbians!"

"When could it have begun? They didn't seem that way when they were with us."

"In that case, it may have begun after they came to Ōmori. I found out entirely by chance."

Eager to discuss it but unable to do so over the phone, Mrs. Harada traveled to Atami that very evening and gave them the whole story. "I don't have any reason to see Mrs. Gamō very often," she said, "but I'm constantly running errands in her neighborhood, so I sometimes pay her a call. Mrs. Gamō tends to go out during the day, though, so I often miss her; perhaps one out of every three visits, those two maids would come to the entrance to tell me, 'Mrs. Gamō is not at home.' This happened so often that I began to notice something strange: they unfailingly came to the entrance together; it was never just one or the other. And it took a surprisingly long time for them to open the door after I rang the bell. Then, one time, the bell was broken, and when I pushed the door, I found it open, so I let myself in and called out for assistance. Setsu came running downstairs from the second floor, all in disarray, and Sayo followed her. Judging by their behavior, I supposed the two of them had taken advantage of their mistress's absence to go up to the second floor somewhere and engage in who-knows-what. After that, out of curiosity, I made it a habit to drop by the Gamō house any time I was in the neighborhood. Then, yesterday, here's what happened. When I tried to ring the bell as usual, it didn't work. I kept pressing it for perhaps five minutes, but it wouldn't ring. Then I tried gently pushing at the door, but it wouldn't open. I had a notion something was up, so I went around to the kitchen entrance very carefully, making as little noise as possible and, finding that door unlocked, I went right in. But there was no one downstairs. On tiptoes, I climbed up to the second floor. The room at the top of the stairs is apparently the master bedroom. Inside, on what must be Mr. and Mrs. Gamō's double bed, I suddenly saw some dreadful form writhing. I can't even say it! Should I call it shameful? Insane? It's too difficult to describe; I'll leave it to your imagination. I was so horrified by what I'd just witnessed that I ran down the stairs, and the two of them, realizing with a cry that I had seen them, jumped up in surprise and tried to cover their lower bodies, but they were both stark naked, so they couldn't easily cover up. Right away, they pulled the duvet over their heads but, when they jerked it up, their four wriggling legs popped out the bottom. For my part, I ran out the kitchen door in a panic, so I don't know what happened after that. I've never seen anything so strange in my life; I thought my heart would never stop pounding." So Mrs. Harada explained.

"What on earth … What time did this happen?"

"Around two clock yesterday—in broad daylight!"

"And you haven't see Mrs. Gamō since?"

"I've been thinking of asking her at some point whether she realizes those two have that sort of relationship, but I was so frightened yesterday that I ran out in a daze. Isn't homosexuality an incredible thing!"

"Shouldn't you hurry and warn her, somehow?"

"They gave me such a menacing look, I was afraid that they might resent me terribly, but, anyway, they know what I saw, so I resigned myself to that and made up my mind to speak to her this morning."

"Over the phone?"

"I couldn't do it over the phone! At first I thought of asking her to come to my house so I could speak to her there, but then if those two were left alone they might do something again, so I went over to Ōmori. And when I did, that woman, the one called Sayo, appeared at the entrance—by herself today—and said, 'Well, ma'am, I do deeply apologize for yesterday. Today, allow me to welcome you properly.' She's brazen."

"Wasn't she glaring at you with those frightening eyes?"

"She was excessively polite, just as always, announcing me in a purring voice, 'Madam, Mrs. Harada is here to see you,' as if nothing had happened—absolutely shameless!"

Mrs. Harada had said to Mrs. Gamō, "We can't talk here. Could we go upstairs?" She was taken to the same room she'd seen yesterday, where she informed her friend of everything she had witnessed, just as it had happened, in sufficient detail. Mrs. Gamō was more shocked than she had expected.

"Why didn't you tell me yesterday that such a thing had happened? Didn't I sleep in this filthy bed last night?!"

"Forgive me! Forgive me! I was so terribly shocked and distressed."

The two ladies sat down in chairs beside the disgusting bed and, for the next two hours, listening carefully for any movements downstairs, gave themselves over to a hushed discussion of how best to handle the situation.

It was not that Mrs. Gamō had been completely inattentive to the situation between the two girls. Once, she had happened to catch a glimpse of them kissing in the kitchen—when had it been?—so it was not as though she'd never wondered if they might be lesbians. She had planned to fire them as soon as she had the chance—it was uncomfortable having two maids involved like that—but it wouldn't be easy to find replacements, so she had continued to use them, thinking all the while, *How unpleasant …*

From what she had observed, it somehow seemed that Setsu took the male role, while Sayo played the female. She thought so, she said, because Setsu had a gaunt, bony body, and Sayo's bearing and manner of speech were lazy and slurred, her skin seemed to suffer from a hormone deficiency, and her hands and feet were rough and dry. Still, as long as they did their work diligently, she had thought, she could put up with them for the time being; as long as it was just between the two of them and didn't inconvenience anyone else, she had decided to close her eyes to it. Even if a lesbian relationship had occurred to her, she said, she never imagined that they were involved carnally in such an indecent way—that things had developed so far!

What follows is an approximation of the conversation between Mrs. Harada and Mrs. Gamō:

"When I took on Sayo, I wondered if I should ask Mrs. Chikura first, but you told me there was no need, and I thought, *That makes sense, since she had been fired for displeasing Mr. Chikura*. But the circumstances were different in Setsu's case, so perhaps it was a mistake to hire her without leave."

"If you put it that way, I suppose I bear some responsibility too, but what does that matter now? It's no longer any concern of the Chikuras. The question is, how do you plan to deal with those two?"

"Lend me a hand. Before we do anything else, I have to deal with this." And with that, she stuck her head out the window and spit—*ptui*!—then picked up the duvet with the tips of her fingers, as though it were something filthy, and tossed it down into the garden.

"Now, Mrs. Harada, you said yourself that you bear some responsibility. Get that end of the mattress and I'll take this end."

"What do you want to do with it?"

"I'm going to throw this thing down into the garden."

Pillows, sheets, mattresses—they all rained down from the second floor onto the lawn.

"I'll call the old man who does the gardening and get him to douse it all with kerosene and burn it!"

"Don't get so agitated! What if you start a fire?"

"I won't be able to shake this feeling of disgust unless I see it burn with my own eyes!"

"Have it taken to the dump."

"I'll sell the bedframe to a secondhand store. It's got to be taken away today!"

"You won't be able to get a new bedframe by tonight …"

"Then I'll sleep with the children downstairs."

When all this uproar was finished, it came time to give the lesbian couple their notice. Mrs. Harada, having been told that she "bore some responsibility," went first down the stairs. When she peeked into the maids' room, both Sayo and Setsu had packed all their bags and trunks neatly in anticipation and were seated in careful composure.

"Here," Mrs. Harada said. "That should cover this month's pay," and taking two sealed envelopes from Mrs. Gamō, she handed them over, one to each girl.

"You understand?"

"Yes."

"Shall I call a car?" This time, Mrs. Gamō spoke.

"It's terribly selfish of me to ask, I know," Sayo replied, "but we have a great deal of luggage. May I beg your permission to use the front gate, ma'am?"

"Be my guest."

"I regret that I could not be of any assistance to you, ma'am; rather, I became a burden to you in many ways, and for that I humbly beg your forgiveness. Mrs. Gamō, Mrs. Harada, please accept my best wishes."

Setsu, as expected, said not a word, but simply walked out awkwardly after Sayo.

Once the car had picked them up and left, Mrs. Gamō called the maid agency immediately and asked them to send a new girl over as quickly as possible. And with that, the whole affair was settled—at least as far as the Gamō household was concerned.

I suppose the two, after being ejected from the house, spent the night together somewhere—perhaps in some cheap hotel—but they couldn't have spent too many nights like that. Nor were they likely to find another situation as convenient as the last, where they could be hired together. It seems that Setsu gave up after a few days and returned to her hometown in Kagoshima. I'm sure that when she left Tokyo her parting with Sayo was tearful, but folks in the Chikura household were relieved to hear how it ended. "It's just as well," they said. "Setsu got involved with the wrong sort; and if she has finally left that woman, then it turned out for the best. She'll soon forget all about that lesbian business." A little later, news reached Raikichi and the others that Setsu had made a good match and remarried, and had a child with her new husband. That was two or three years ago.

As for Sayo, there was a rumor that she had returned to Atami and was working as the housemother at a dormitory somewhere while receiving treatment for a skin condition, but Raikichi and the others never went to see her. For some reason, though, she occasionally sent letters to Mrs. Gamō, and gifts of pickled radish. Then, one day, unexpectedly, a parcel arrived with a return address in Tokushima, Sayo's hometown. When Mrs. Gamō opened it, out tumbled one glove, as black as if it had been rubbed in cinders, an old sukiyaki pot, and a pile of other rubbish. Finally a postcard fell out with the message, "God told me to return these to you, so here they are."

Chapter Ten

KOMA WAS THE ONLY ONE OF THE GIRLS NOT RAISED in the countryside. She had been born in Kyoto and came into service through a recommendation from the kimono-maker. Koma had a long face with a pointy chin. She called herself "Kao Soap" because she resembled the brand's logo—a face shaped like a crescent moon—and whenever a TV show started with the announcement that it was "sponsored by Kao Soap," she would say, "That's my program!" I've already mentioned her strange habit of getting the dry heaves. Well, something else strange happened once, when she went with Mutsuko to the movie theater in Atami to see that Disney movie called *The Living Desert.* They found separate seats in different parts of the theater, but when a creature like a giant centipede appeared on screen, a retching sound rang through the theater, and then someone ran toward the rest rooms in a panic, covering her mouth. Mutsuko swiveled her head around thinking "That must be Koma," and, sure enough, it was.

What that creature was exactly, I don't know—some sort of reptile, apparently, about one meter long—but it didn't take such a big thing to upset Koma; even a mouse scuffling around the kitchen or a little worm crawling on the ceiling nauseated her. The Chikuras liked cats and always kept one—Persian, Siamese, or domestic—and it was a maid's job to clean out the litter box. Koma did everything she could to avoid that task, but when she got stuck with it, working the late shift, you could hear the sound of her retching coming from the kitchen in the middle of the night.

That wasn't so bad, but she would also retch at mealtime when she saw some food that she hated set out on the table, or saw someone eating it. She was disgusted by French toast, which Gin loved, and whenever she saw Gin eating it, Koma would cry as she ran for the toilet, "I don't know how you can eat such a thing!"

Although she got over it later, for some time after she came into service, Koma couldn't handle beef. Whenever it was her job to do the carving, she would cover her mouth and nose with a towel tied tight as a gag, or wear a contraption that looked like a muzzle for a mad dog, and then she'd take the very biggest knife in one hand and, in the other, a long, long set of kitchen chopsticks, and prod the meat from as far away as possible. In that absurd getup, she looked just like someone setting out on a mission of vengeance, and Sanko, coming upon her, wondered what in the world was going on. Koma also hated thrusting her hand deep into the pickling bran to turn the pickles. Instead of using her hand, she'd use the rice paddle or a set of kitchen chopsticks and hastily give the pickles a stir so that, when the job was left to her, the eggplant turned yellow and was hardly pickled at all. Sanko and Nioko scolded her constantly: "The bran always goes bad when you do the pickles!"

With her various other strange habits, Koma figured in many bizarre episodes. Once, one of the weekly magazines made a big fuss over the issue of artificial insemination. This was just at the time when Raikichi was prostrate with high blood pressure and attended by a nurse. One evening, it seems, while sharing the bath with this nurse, Koma asked her with a grave face, "What drug store can I go to for some semen?" We all laughed when we heard it.

Generally speaking, she was shockingly ignorant about sexual matters. When she saw two dogs copulating, she thought the smaller one was being bullied and said, "Poor thing! Let's help her out." Once the real situation was explained to her, she became very curious about the subject, and whenever she heard that two dogs were going at it, she would go to watch. Since she was so naive, it was hardly surprising that until recently she had been under the impression that babies were born from their mother's belly. At one time, she even believed that men and women could make a baby simply by kissing; she'd also thought that roosters could lay eggs. At first, Sanko suspected her of playing dumb, but she was dead serious. Because she was so naive about such things, Koma didn't marry until quite late, remaining with the Chikuras while girls who had come to work in the house after her married and left. She was twenty when she came into service and thirty-two when she made a good match at last, so she worked for them for over a decade.

When a wedding date was finally set, Sanko started to worry about how Koma would handle her wedding night, so she took down a carefully guarded volume of woodblock prints by Hokusai or Toyokuni and furtively opened it to show the girl. Koma screamed in panic, clasped Sanko around the knees, and began to tremble like a leaf, so that Sanko staggered and almost fell over. Koma's face turned bright red. "I feel a little strange," she said. Almost immediately however she made an effort to control her breathing and then, after staring fixedly at the pictures, she continued, "But I like looking at this sort of thing." Ordinarily, you wouldn't say such a thing out loud, even if you felt that way, but Koma wasn't the sort to keep anything to herself.

Once, she complained of a stomach ache and asked, "Madam, please call the doctor. I think I have dysentery."

"Did you eat something bad?"

"My stomach hurts like crazy. Just now, I went to the bathroom, and so much blood came out, I'm sure it must be dysentery." She seemed to be in great pain. When the doctor examined her, though, it turned out to be no more than her period and cramps. She had thrown the household into an uproar, but once she heard this she acted as though nothing had happened, saying nonchalantly, "It's just my time of the month."

She often suffered from cramps, and at those times she would tear wildly at the tatami mats on the floor, screaming, "Mommy! Help me!"

Once, when she was a child, she'd announced, "I'm going to jump from the second floor and kill myself." None of the adults took her seriously, so no one responded, and they were all dumbfounded when she really did jump. "I don't care if I die," she used to say, and, "If anyone wanted to die—if they wanted to die, but they were afraid to kill themself—I'd kill them without a second thought. If a person wants to die, then killing them is a kindness, isn't it?" In her case, it was quite possible that she meant it in all earnest. One day Mutsuko, suffering from nervous depression, said, "I just want to die!" Hearing that, Koma told her, "If you really wish to die, Miss, I can arrange it so you won't even notice when it happens." Mutsuko was a bit creeped out.

Koma would become so obsessed with some chore that she would wake up in the middle of the night and begin to do it. She'd be in the kitchen all night long, rustling around as she tidied up, until the other maids were at their wits' end from lack of sleep. Mutsuko taught her to knit, and once she started a piece, she'd work through the night to finish it. After Mutsuko got married, she began knitting various items for her future baby, and Koma was constantly by her side, knitting something herself so that, even before she met her future husband, she had completed all sorts of caps, capes, and socks for their baby.

Before coming into service, she had been enrolled in a teacher-training course at a private handicraft school for girls, where she had joined the theater department. She hadn't really studied anything there, though, because that was in the middle of the war. After graduating, she went to work at the Fujii-Daimaru department store in the Shijō area of Kyoto. She joined their company theater troupe too and, so she said, worked hard to perfect her standard Japanese in order to compete against troupes from other department stores. Perhaps that's why she was so extremely talented at mimicking people's voices and manners of speech.

One day—this was after Raikichi had moved from the Nakada house to a cottage near Narusawa, halfway up Mount Izu, where the statue of the Kōa Kannon stands—Koma was alone at home with Mutsuko when they heard something suspicious outside. Frightened, Mutsuko said, "I wonder if somebody's out there?" Koma opened the window beside the front door just a crack and, throwing her voice, impersonated five or six people, men and women, having an absurd conversation. She used comical voices, a completely different one for each person, wittily coming up with a variety of topics—you've never heard such clever variations. She used all sorts of techniques to alter her voice—pinching her nose, pulling the skin of her throat. She'd pretend to answer the phone in a high-pitched voice, and could make it sound as though five or six people were clamoring down a hallway and then, in contrast, mimic the sound of someone walking in a dignified manner. She did it all more for her own amusement than to trick any burglars.

Best of all was her impression of a gorilla. She was too shy ever to perform this trick in front of Raikichi and Sanko no matter how often they asked, but in front of Mutsuko or the other maids, or the neighborhood children, she'd sometimes get carried away and put on a show. Her terrifying expression was so lifelike that some of the children would begin to whimper and cry. Her mouth was so pliable that she could stuff a whole apple into each cheek and alter her features however she pleased. To mimic a gorilla, she would first of all stuff her whole tongue under her upper lip, then draw the lip down as much as possible over it. Then she'd cross her eyes like Ben Turpin, the old-time American comedian, and next, she'd throw both arms open and spread her hands wide, curling the fingertips. Then, wrapping something like a diaper around herself, she would stand bandy-legged.

Koma was also very skilled at the hula dance. There was one other person in Atami known for the hula, the owner of a restaurant called Wakana, whom Raikichi and his wife had seen perform a few times at banquets, but everyone agreed that Koma was the better hula dancer.

It had long been Koma's wish to see herself on television. At that time, there was a program on the Nippon Television Network called "Fashion Classroom." The hostess, a beautician named Nawa Yoshiko, would choose one woman at random from among the hopefuls in the audience and give her a flattering new hairstyle before bringing her back out. It happened that Sanko was on friendly terms with Nawa Yoshiko going back to the days when she'd run a beauty parlor in the Daimaru department store in Kobe, and so was able to request a ticket to the show for Koma. Unfortunately, Koma wasn't selected, and so she was unable to realize her dream. Fuji Television also had a program at that time, hosted by the famous silent-film narrator Tokugawa Musei, called "Television Wedding." Koma often said how she hoped to appear on the program when she got married, and since Sensei must know Tokugawa Musei, perhaps he could intercede on her behalf, and so on. There was no way to make this happen, though, and Raikichi paid her no attention. A bit later, the Matsuzaka department store in Tokyo installed a camera in their store so that customers could watch themselves on a closed-circuit TV as they rode the up escalator. It was probably installed to promote television sets, but Koma was thrilled to be broadcast on a TV right before her own eyes, and she rode the escalator again and again, watching herself.

She also had a habit of talking in her sleep at great length. She would scold the dog in her sleep, or talk about dancing. She would doze off in the bath after working the late shift and, rowing as though she was in a boat, plunge her face into the hot water and wake up with a start. Yet another of her habits was leaving her umbrella or handbag behind when she got out of a car or off a train or bus. One umbrella was supposed to be left in the kitchen for all the maids to use, but the others complained, "Koma always leaves the kitchen umbrella behind on the bus."

She was a fan of foreign films and knew quite a number of the actors' names. She was partial to Ben Johnson, the star of westerns, and would send him Christmas cards and fan letters written in Japanese, getting Mutsuko to address the envelope in English for her, and when one day a reply came from Johnson with a publicity photo enclosed, she hung it on her wall.

Koma's father was an eccentric too—old-fashioned, stubborn, with a strong sense of duty. He had graduated from the design department in the school of fine arts that once stood where the University of Arts is now. The silk-dyeing houses commissioned him to come up with designs for scarfs, neckties, wrapping cloths, and the like. He wasn't in dire straits, but he was a soft touch and couldn't refuse people who asked for a loan, and so he impoverished himself by paying off other people's debts. When he sent his daughter into service with the Chikura household, he told her in no uncertain terms: No matter how difficult things might become, you're to serve Raikichi-sensei and the madam loyally; if you ever leave the Chikura house and return home, my door will be shut to you, so you might as well throw yourself into Lake Biwa and drown. The letters that he sometimes sent to his daughter always included these admonitions, bulleted and carefully underlined in red: "Beware of fire. Lock your doors. Be careful in traffic." Sometimes Koma would ask for time off to visit her father, but when she did, he would hurry her off as the time approached for her return to the Chikura house. In one of the letters he sent her, the father had written along the edge, "I suppose the household keeps several dogs as pets. Dogs are unable to tell people what they need, so you should sympathize with them and treat them kindly." Overwhelmed with work, Koma hadn't had a moment to think about the dogs but, reading this, she suddenly remembered them. Two, named Suke and Kaku, had recently run away into the mountains behind the house.* It was quite usual for the two of them to head up the mountain toward the statue of Kannon and later return covered in fleas. Feeling that she had disappointed both the dogs and her father, Koma immediately went to search for them. She returned triumphantly with the two dogs, then spent the next three hours picking fleas off and crushing them. She counted the fleas out of habit, and they amounted to five thousand. She wept fat tears as she crushed each of the five thousand fleas against a stone. She couldn't control herself—her own heartlessness angered her so. How many fleas the poor dogs had collected all over their bodies! That's why she cried; the poor dogs looked so pathetic, she could hardly stand it.

Koma was her father's daughter, a soft touch and honest to a fault, just like him. When asked for a loan by one of the other maids or the young people who came to the house regularly, she would often go to great lengths to collect some money, only to get angry later when they forgot to repay her.

---

* The dogs are named for two characters from the popular tale of the Tokugawa official Mito Kōmon.—Tr.

Chapter Eleven

NOW, LET ME BRIEFLY INTRODUCE A GIRL NAMED
Suzu (or "Bell"), who arrived three or four years after Koma. Suzu
came to us through the offices of the same kimono-maker who had
recommended Koma—not that the Chikura household was short of
maids or had sought out this woman's help. That woman came to the
house in Shimogamo one day and said, "Madam, madam! It doesn't
look as though you're short-staffed, but could you by any chance use
another maid? I happen to know of a very lovely girl, and I wouldn't
feel right placing her with just any household. I'd be so grateful if
you could use her here." And so, one way or another, it was settled.

Raikichi still remembers it exactly. He had just suffered his first
stroke, a mild one that left the right side of his body slightly im-
paired, and for a couple of years he was confined to bed periodically;
that was between the spring of 1952 and fall of 1954. After that first
stroke occurred at a Tokyo inn, he was transported back to Atami
but then, feeling no better, he steeled himself against the winter cold

and returned to Kyoto around October of 1952. After arriving at the station, he was carried from the platform and over the bridge with some difficulty, then taken by car up to the front gate of the house in the Forest of Correction. Again, two people, one under each arm, helped him to the Japanese-style room at the back, where he was so dizzy he couldn't sit up. He was lifted into a bed that had been readied for him, and there he passed day after lonely day, gazing at the stones and the fountain in the autumn-deepened garden and listening to the clack of the bamboo water-tipper. Then, one day, Sanko drew close to his pillow and said, "There's a new girl coming, and I hear she's very pretty. They say she looks just like the actress Tsushima Keiko."

It wasn't that Raikichi and his wife required exceptionally pretty girls as maids. After all, those they had employed for so many years hadn't been especially pretty; nevertheless, it was a fact that Raikichi's gloomy depression dissipated when he heard Sanko say this, and the world he looked out upon seemed gradually to brighten. For he had begun to wonder when he would be well enough to get out of bed and take a turn in the garden or walk with a cane through the sacred grove in the grounds of Shimogamo Shrine—or whether perhaps he would never get out of bed again. Though he had come home to his beloved Kyoto, he was unable to visit his old haunts in Gion, Kawaramachi, and Saga in Arashiyama, never mind Yase and Ōhara. He might be dead before the winter; who knew? So when, just as he was beginning to have such thoughts, this beautiful girl materialized to look after him morning and night, it eased his heart immeasurably. Though he didn't say so, Raikichi wasn't particularly partial to Tsushima Keiko—in his situation, however, it was enough just to have a pretty girl around.

If you take the Kōjaku Railroad from Ōtsu in Shiga prefecture past Katata Station, near the "floating temple" of Mangetsu-ji, the next stop is a station called Mano. It is a shore village with an ancient history, about which Princess Shikishi long ago wrote the poem:

The chill of the midnight shore wind blowing. At the inlets around
Mano Bay, now I hear the plover cry.

And the Buddhist priest Sosen wrote:

In the wind that sweeps the cloud from Mount Hira, the moon is clear.
The icy waves of Mano Bay.

Suzu was the daughter of a farming family from this village. Raikichi had never been to Mano, but he had traveled to the area around
Chino in Yokawa, at the foot of Mount Hiei, to search for material
for his writing, and had visited the Ogoto hot springs nearby, so he
had a rough idea of the place. He was partial somehow to that sort
of landscape. She had arrived on a clear, brisk afternoon, dressed in
a carmine *meisen* silk kimono with a yellow and green *tatewaku* pattern and a *haori* jacket with a green ground and a pinwheel pattern
of yellow, grey, and carmine (she liked that color, and it suited her
well). Her hair was done in the O-kappa style, and her sash was a soft,
youthful *heko-obi*. She was twenty-one.

In those days, girls who came to job interviews typically wore
plain western-style clothes—handknit sweaters and the like—so
the sight of Suzu, absolutely lovely in her silk kimono, captivated
him. Her father was descended from an old Shiga farming family,
and her mother had been born into a Kyoto merchant house. The
mother had moved to Mano when she married and had struggled
at first with the unfamiliar life of the farm. Of course a mother like
that would have put special effort into the personal appearance of
such a pretty daughter.

Suzu called the kimono-maker "aunt Kodama." On the day of the
interview, her "aunt" brought Suzu on the streetcar to the terminal at
Demachi, where they alighted and began to cross the Kawai Bridge
over the Kamo River, toward the approach to Shimogamo Shrine.
Something must have occurred suddenly to the older woman half-

way across the bridge, for she stopped and said, "You can't go to an interview with your face powdered like that," and, taking out her own compact from the folds of her sash, she rubbed all the powder from Suzu's face. When Suzu appeared before Raikichi and his wife, her face was simple and free of makeup.

Raikichi's sickroom was ringed by a veranda on the east and south sides, with a pond beyond the handrails into which a waterfall spilled. It should have been quite a bright and cheerful room, but, in keeping with the old-fashioned abhorrence of direct sunlight, a trellis had been hung from the eaves down to the surface of the pond and the branches of a dense evergreen vine trained to it, so the room was gloomy even on a bright day. When Suzu was brought into the room by Sanko to meet him, Raikichi was lying on his stomach, his face turned to one side on the pillow, drinking bitter persimmon juice. The juice was sold at a shop with a long history called Shibuya that stood (and no doubt still stands) on Kawaramachi Street, just above Marutamachi, on the west side of the road. Now that he had been brought home from Atami, the important thing for Raikichi was to drink bitter persimmon juice to reduce his blood pressure, and someone had told them "the juice from Shibuya is the best — by all means, try drinking some and see," so he was testing it out, one cup twice daily in the morning and evening, as directed. It wasn't a particularly pleasant taste, so after drinking it down straight, he immediately rinsed his mouth with a cup of water. Later on, Suzu told Raikichi that when she had come into the room and seen a weak, decrepit old man stretched out on the bed in that gloomy, dark room, grimacing as he drank his juice, he looked so miserable and pathetic that she thought to herself, *Do I really have to live here as this old man's companion? What a terrible place to enter into service!* Raikichi was sixty-eight at the time, and ill, so it's not surprising that he looked like an old man; he very likely looked even older than usual. Thank goodness, by March or April, after that winter had passed, Raikichi's health began gradually to improve and by May he was able to walk not only to the Forest of Correction but occasionally as far as Kawaramachi. The color of his skin had improved notably by then, too, and he had regained the strength in his legs, so that Suzu suddenly revised her opinion of him, deciding he wasn't such a frightful old man after all, and as he continued to improve day by day she was surprised to find that he looked more like a man in his fifties, she said.

On the other side of the pond, across an earthen bridge, was a small outbuilding that had been given the name "Gōkantei," or "the pavilion of shared pleasure." Raikichi had made one of its rooms into his study and started little by little to work there, but whenever he fell idle, he would eagerly summon Suzu, sit her on the other side of his desk, and make her practice her letters. Anything might serve as a copybook — a magazine lying about, or a novel — but he always chose something with the simplest sentences; then he would read aloud as she listened. Suzu would open a cheap paper notepad and copy it down with an HB pencil. Her penmanship was shockingly poor. Perhaps it was to be expected of such a country girl, but she had graduated middle school, after all, and yet she was still quite untrained in writing. You'd think that her school wasn't very good, or that she was simply born with a poor memory, but neither was the case. After inquiring in various ways, he learned that Suzu had worked in the fields in place of her city-born mother, often missing school in the busy season and inevitably neglecting her studies. So now her priority was not to improve her handwriting but simply to learn to read and write at least a few more characters, and she endeavored to memorize one new *kanji* each day, practicing the proper stroke order in pencil (learning to write with a brush was less important to her).

"There's no question that girl is pretty but, sadly, there's no sparkle in her eyes," Sanko often said. "If they showed some keenness, some flash of insight, she'd be a real beauty. You could even recommend her as an actress. If only she'd been sent to a better school, given some refinement, then those eyes would certainly have some radiance."

Husband and wife had betrayed similar thoughts regarding Hatsu, and now once again they were made to feel the impossibility of ever knowing at just what a disadvantage these girls were, compared to their counterparts in the city, simply because they'd lacked access to a good education.

The lessons in the study didn't continue for very long. For a while, Raikichi taught Suzu daily, for about thirty minutes to an hour, less for her benefit than as a way of dissipating the gloom that plagued his own heart, but with the first buds of spring Raikichi's condition improved, and he discontinued the lessons once he was able to leave the house on his own. Over that month or two, though, just think how much comfort Raikichi took from the lessons! Nor did Suzu spend that time with him in vain. She worked for the Chikura household for five or six years more, and one day, Raikichi happened to notice a draft of a letter that she had thrown away. He was struck by the elegance of the handwriting.

"Did Suzu really write this?!"

"That's right," Sanko replied, "Suzu really wrote it! You know, back when you were giving her lessons, she would shut herself up in the maids' room and practice the characters you'd taught her countless times, and even after the lessons ended, I'd see her practicing in secret whenever she had a spare moment, writing the characters in the air with her finger. What do you think? Did you ever suppose she would become so skillful?"

Raikichi was more than a little surprised to see how much Suzu's calligraphy had improved in just a few years; the letter looked as though it had been written by a completely different person—the difficult *kanji* flowing one after another in a smooth line. It pained him to think what a splendid young lady she would have made, judging by this evidence, if only she had attended high school. Still, she had good arms and legs, despite having worked in the countryside as a child; they weren't wiry or knotted. And while her bust was well developed—rounded and firm—her overall figure was slim and graceful. The only real fault in her looks were the callouses on her ankles from sitting Japanese-style. In the old days, you'd see these on almost any Japanese person, man or woman. Raikichi had them too. The ugly traces of being made to sit respectfully on the floor—feet tucked under one's backside, in student lodgings or a tiny cram-school classroom—they were gradually becoming unusual among the ill-mannered postwar generation. How unfortunate, then, to see them on this girl. There was one more thing: her hair was streaked with strands of gray and reddish-brown. This probably had something to do with her poor diet as a child; after she came to live in the Chikura household, these decreased little by little until she was left at last with a gorgeous head of pure black hair that delighted her family and neighbors when she went home to visit.

Blessed from birth with a highly developed sense of taste, Suzu excelled as a cook because she could discriminate between what tasted good and what did not. No doubt this was also because she'd been trained in the Kansai way of cooking by the veteran maid, Hatsu, who was still working for the Chikura household at the time, going back and forth between Kyoto and Atami and overseeing the kitchens. Even the tea tasted better when Suzu made it. And because of her sensibility, she enjoyed good food more than most people, so Raikichi and Sanko would sometimes take her out to a restaurant where the food was particularly fine or, when they had something special at home, set aside a bit for her, saying, "Here, try this." It was worthwhile to treat her.

That reminds me of a story that people still tell today. Once, just after she'd started working in the Shimogamo house, Suzu entered the Japanese-style room to serve dinner to her master, only to find Raikichi sitting in bed with a serving table set on the mattress. It was a tall-style serving tray, lacquered, with a rectangular top and beveled edges. On the table and on a tray beside it were arranged countless dishes holding foods that Suzu had never seen before and could not even identify. They had been ordered from a Chinese restaurant called Hiun, or "Flying Cloud," that is still doing business at the intersection of Kiyamachi and Sanjō today. As for the dishes, I imagine they included such things as chilled jellyfish, "thousand-year" eggs, and Dongpo pork, swallow's nest soup, and shark fin soup. Seeing the master and mistress evidently enjoying these dishes, Suzu marveled at what strange things there are to eat in this world, and just then Sanko began to serve a little of each dish into a small plate or bowl, saying "Here, Suzu. You've never tasted this sort of thing before, have you? Try a little. If you bring it back to the kitchen, everyone will want some, so eat it here."

And with that, Suzu tasted Chinese food for the first time. Never had she tasted anything so delectable! She wondered, *Can something really be this delicious?* Forever after, she never tired of telling people about the shock she received that day.

Raikichi took her to the restaurant Alaska on the sixth floor of Asahi Hall in Kawaramachi. Ordinarily, a girl unused to the area would have been bewildered and flustered by that sort of dining hall, but Suzu was right at home, unintimidated from the first. One reason may have been that, by virtue of her prettiness, the waiter took her for Raikichi's daughter and treated her accordingly. Taking her place across the table from Raikichi and paying close attention to her master's movements (and, of course, listening to his instructions), she studied every aspect of table manners, from the proper way to eat soup to the use of knife, fork, butter knife, and so on, and did it all without embarrassing him. This was difficult for a maid, but she gained courage from the experience; afterward, she could be taken to even the fanciest place and, without blundering—but likewise, miraculously, without putting on airs—would instinctively discern the atmosphere.

Chapter Twelve

SUZU USUALLY ACCOMPANIED RAIKICHI WHEN HE went for a walk. Calling, "Suzu! Come here!" he would set out suddenly in the evening and, when so inclined, head for some intimate little shop where the food was good—the restaurant Tan-kuma, northwest of the intersection of Kiyamachi-dōri and Shijō-dōri, for example, or Tsubosaka, in Sueyoshi-chō, in Gion—escorting Suzu through the curtain at the entrance. But something happened once at Tsubosaka. Raikichi loved tongue stew and, thinking that Suzu would like it too, ordered two servings. But Suzu gave a worried look and, drawing her mouth close to his ear, whispered, "Sensei, isn't this cow's tongue?"

"That's right. Perhaps you don't like cow's tongue?"

"I will eat anything else, but please forgive me if I don't eat that."

"But why?"

Since her family's home was on the banks of picturesque Lake Biwa, you might well imagine that it was a quiet and refined place, but more and more traffic had been passing on the road in front of their house in recent years, raising clouds of dust. As she worked in the fields, Suzu would watch cows pulling two-wheeled carts along that dusty road, their long tongues lolling out, drooling saliva as they passed, and see the saliva fall, drop by drop, onto the road. That had been a daily sight, so when it occurred to her that she was eating *that* tongue, Suzu felt sick and lost her appetite.

When in Tokyo, they mainly went to one of two Chinese food shops, Shinbashi-tei in Shinbashi or Shinya Hanten in Tamurachō, and, for Japanese food, to Tsujitome in the food-basement of the Daimaru department store, or Hamasaku in West Ginza, or the like. Mind you, in Tokyo, it was seldom just the two of them; often they were joined by two or three members of the family. And it wasn't as though Suzu was designated as Raikichi's sole companion; other maids sometimes accompanied him. Still, it was most often Suzu. The other maids didn't eat the same food as the family; they were provided with simple dishes, suitable for maids. In Suzu's case, though, Raikichi would sometimes tell the chef, "This girl loves good food and knows about cooking, so please serve her whatever she wants."

Suzu came to us in the fall of 1952, and at the end of March of the following year, a girl named Gin (or "Silver") arrived. Gin was nineteen at the time, three years younger than Suzu, and the youngest maid living in the Chikura house. She came recommended by Hatsu and was the first girl in a while from Kagoshima. According to Hatsu, Gin was the daughter of the family across the road from her own house. While Hatsu's family was terribly poor, Gin's family owned considerable property and lived in some comfort—a completely different standard of living from Hatsu's family—and as the daughter of such a family, Gin could have continued on to high school, but she hadn't wanted to. Hatsu recommended her as an honest and clever girl who could be useful if the family wanted her, so she came to us.

Suzu and this girl Gin were the two real beauties among all the maids who worked for the Chikura household. Suzu had the sort of beauty that appealed to everyone; no one who saw her would dispute it. Gin's beauty, on the other hand, was perhaps more a matter of preference. Raikichi's own taste declared Gin the more beautiful, but not until two or three years after she started working here. When she first came to interview, he couldn't have imagined that her face would become so lovely. Only—from the beginning—her eyes were big and round and full of charm, and surprisingly expressive.

"What eyes that girl has!" Sanko had said immediately. In this aspect, Gin was quite distinct from Suzu, and possessed something that the other girl lacked.

Soon after Gin came into service, she was involved in two memorable incidents. I've already explained that, in the Chikura household, maids were given an alias for work because of an old-fashioned notion that it was discourteous to a girl's parents to use her real name. In fact, "Koma," "Sada," and "Suzu" were not those girls' real names. So, when Gin joined the household, she too was given an alias, in keeping with this custom. *What shall we call her,* the master and his family wondered. *How about this or that,* they said, until it was decided that "Ume" (or "Plum") would do.

The thing is, the other Ume who had worked for the family previously (whose real name had been Kuni, or "Nation") had been born and raised in Kagoshima as well, after all, and besides, she had a distant family connection with Gin: it seems that the first Ume was Gin's aunt's niece, and after her father's untimely death, she had been taken in by Gin's family and raised by them until, upon finishing middle school, she was sent into service in Kyoto. Later, due to her unfortunate condition, she had asked the Chikura family to let her leave service and return to her hometown, but then the condition had turned out not to be that serious, and she was now healthy. Given their connection, it was decided that Gin should take the same alias that Kuni had used.

When Sanko went to inform the girl herself of her new name, however, she responded quite frankly, "I'd rather not, ma'am."

"Whyever not?"

"I don't want to take the name of someone with epilepsy," she said. "My name is Gin, so that will do. Please call me by my real name."

Her manner of speech was quite brusque, and at that moment Raikichi and Sanko thought: *This Gin has a willful streak*. Sanko's younger sister, Nioko, had set up house in Nishi-Shirakawa after being widowed and needed a maid, so she borrowed Gin from her older sister, but Gin returned to the Chikura household after just one day, saying, "I came here with the understanding that I would be working for Chikura-sensei."

A little stream ran in a trickle north to south in front of the gate to the Shimogamo house. Some say this is the "cicada stream" mentioned in the old poem by Kamo no Chōmei, but Yoshida Tōgo clearly contradicts this in his dictionary of place-names, and the local people call the stream Izumigawa. It has its source in the village of Matsugasaki and flows down east of the Forest of Correction before meeting the river that runs through Kyoto, the Kamo. When the maids of the Chikura household went out to do their shopping, they would cross a simple bridge that spanned this stream in front of the house, walk west across the road that leads through the grove to the shrine, and come out on the street where the bus for Midorogaike runs (the streetcar hadn't yet reached that neighborhood). About that bridge: there had been a crude earthen bridge there, but after that was washed away, the people in the neighborhood pooled their money to replace it with one made of concrete. I say concrete, but it was a simple thing, one meter wide and about six meters long, with no railing, inclining slightly from each end toward the middle to form a low arch. It was a bit dangerous to ride one's bicycle over it, so most people would dismount at the edge of the bridge and walk their bicycle over, but returning home from an errand one day, Gin, with youthful confidence, tried to ride over the bridge and fell, bicycle and all, into the stream.

This happened at around two in the afternoon. The stream was very shallow, so there was no danger of her drowning, but Gin hit her forehead hard on some of the broken crockery that littered the stream bed, and blood was gushing from her brow. Koma was just walking out of the front gate and heading toward the stream when Gin stumbled up the bank, blood dripping down her face.

"Oh no! Gin, what happened?!"

Gin didn't answer her, saying only "I left the shopping basket in the river. Would you go and get it? There's cash in it."

"Never mind about the cash! First let's take care of that cut."

Koma carried the girl, bloody from head to toe, into the kitchen and called a taxi.

"I'm sorry," she was told, "but no regular taxis are available currently, only a large one."

"A large one is fine, only send it quick!" Having done this, she stepped out of the front door with Gin to discover that the neighbors, wondering what was up, had gathered in a noisy crowd. The taxi was too big for the narrow road, and the driver had to stop some distance from the front gate. Blinded by the blood streaming down her face, Gin staggered between the people, jumped into the taxi, and immediately covered herself so no one could see her through the window.

Koma, jumping in after her, said, "To Kōori Hospital, on Ōike Road!"

While Gin continued to sob tearfully, she never once complained of the pain. Rather, concerned about her appearance, she was saying, "Look how filthy I am!" and "My kimono is covered with mud!" and "I'm ashamed to be seen like this."

Honestly, she looked as though she had just come out of the river, blood still trickling steadily from her wet and sticky clothes and dripping all over the taxi.

Upon examination at the hospital, the gash in Gin's forehead turned out to be three centimeters long. She was immediately administered penicillin and an injection to prevent tetanus, then she was given a local anesthetic, and the cut was sewn shut. When she returned home, her face had swollen to more than twice its size, and it was wrapped around and around with a bandage. She had a fever of nearly 104.

"What a thing to happen!" Sanko exclaimed. "What will I tell your mother when she sees that cut on your forehead!"

"Please don't concern yourself, ma'am. This is entirely my fault and no one else's. It has nothing to do with you. I should have gotten off my bicycle, but I stupidly tried to ride it across the bridge," Gin replied. "That's why this has happened, and that's just what I'll tell my mother."

The stubborn girl tried to go right back to work, braving the fever and with her head still wrapped in bandages, but the master and mistress scolded her severely, and she acquiesced. She returned to the hospital several times to get further shots of penicillin, and even now, already nine years since the incident, there remains a faint trace of the gash on her forehead. Once you're used to it, you hardly notice, but I suppose some people think it a shame, since her face is so lovely. In any case, she'll certainly carry that scar for the rest of her life.

Well then, why don't we return now to Hatsu's story?

When Hatsu recommended Gin, in 1953, she had already been working for the Chikura household for eighteen years, included the war years, during which she had traveled back to her hometown several times—when her mother had fallen ill, for instance, and when her brother had died from tuberculosis. She had been twenty when she came to work at the Tantaka-bayashi house in 1936, and she was now almost forty years old. Sad to say, she had not received a single suitable offer of marriage from anyone, either in Kyoto or her hometown.

Once, while they were living at the house in Teramachi-Imadegawa, Raikichi was walking with her around Kawaramachi when Hatsu stopped suddenly and looked him in the eye. "Sensei, do you think I'll ever get married?" She seemed to be truly at a loss.

"Oh, you will," Raikichi answered at the time. "Of course you will—so there's no need to worry." He believed that while most people might consider a girl like Hatsu homely, not everyone would. Let me review Hatsu's good points, as I first described them in Chapter 2. There, I said that "When Mutsuko compared [Hatsu] to McDaniel, she was thinking only of the shape of her face; her skin was snow white. Her figure was ample and well developed, but not sloppy. She was taller than average for a twenty-year-old woman of that time, almost thirty years ago, and fit. Her fingers were long, and her feet, though quite big, were not badly shaped. And though Raikichi hadn't seen her naked, according to Mutsuko, her bust was 'better than Marilyn Monroe's,'" and I continued, "Raikichi hated to see a woman with dirty soles, and the soles of Hatsu's feet always looked smooth and pure white, as though she had just scrubbed them with a washcloth. If you happened to peer down into her collar, you'd find her underclothes freshly washed and impeccably clean." So you see, when Raikichi told her, "Of course you'll get married," he was not merely trying to console her; he really thought she would. If a girl like Hatsu couldn't find someone to take her as a bride, then the men of the world were just too stubborn, that was all. A suitable prospect was bound to turn up before long—he was sure of it. Somehow, though, no one ever had.

Hatsu was left to look after the Atami house on her own for some time and it seems that she occasionally invited over some of the young deliverymen who were constantly in and out, treating them to sukiyaki and staying up late with them. Raikichi and Sanko heard about this from someone soon afterward. *Perhaps Hatsu can't bear it any longer*, they worried between themselves; *she's a fastidious woman at heart and, up until now, she hasn't slipped up even once; let's hope she hasn't fallen in with a bad crowd and strayed.* Fortunately, she was soon summoned from Atami back to Kyoto and sent to work for the Asukai household in Kita-Shirakawa, and it all came to an end without any damage to her reputation.

After her husband, Asukai Jirō, died of cancer in 1949, Nioko, now a widow, had sold the house in Nanzenji and moved back in for a little while with her older sister, Sanko, at Shimogamo and, since she had no children of her own, she made Keisuke, Sanko's son by her former husband, her own heir. With that, Keisuke was able to marry for love—he wed a girl named Numeko, a graduate of the English department at Dōshisha University, and Nioko had a house built for them near the flower garden behind the Kita-Shirakawa house, in the ruins of the ancient Shirakawa palace. Hatsu went to work there just as this young couple was welcoming a new daughter, Miyuki, and were very much in need of her assistance.

Numeko shared the blood of her grandfather—the famous painter Nashimoto Ransetsu—and was a brilliant girl with an edge like a sharp knife. She was quite a demanding and reserved young mistress, but she never had a single complaint about Hatsu and still feels deeply grateful for all Hatsu's work. No doubt, one reason for that gratitude was that, in contrast to the twenty-four year old Numeko, Hatsu, her senior by thirteen or fourteen years, was competent at everything, even though she had no children of her own. Familiar with housekeeping and of course caring for children, and completely at home cooking for a family, she must have been a treasure in many ways. I suppose Hatsu's big-framed and generous physique and her easygoing, calm, and confidently bossy personality had a gently soothing effect on the high-strung young Numeko. The sight of baby Miyuki, snuggled deep in Hatsu's big arms, fast asleep, would, I think, give anyone a feeling of reassurance and reliability.

Chapter Thirteen

AT THAT TIME — THAT IS, WHEN SHE WAS LOOKING
after Miyuki and helping with the Asukai family's housekeeping—Hatsu unexpectedly received two matchmaking propositions
from completely different sources: one through the masseuse who
was constantly working on Raikichi's legs and back and the other
through Hatsu's older sister in Wakayama.

The man in question in the case of the masseuse was the owner of
a pharmacy who lived near the intersection of Senbon and Shimo-
tachiuri avenues in Kyoto. His first wife had died, so this would be his
second marriage, but he had no children. His lifestyle was not very
luxurious, but, anyway, he lived comfortably. The masseuse did not
know him personally—there was another go-between involved—
but it pained her to think that Hatsu might spend her whole life
alone, she said, and so she had brought the prospect to them out of
the goodness of her heart.

As for the other prospect, the one that came through Wakayama:
I mentioned before that Hatsu's sister was living there; well, the sister

was pursuing the alliance on both Hatsu's account and her own. She had allowed herself to be sold into service and sent to Wakayama in exchange for an advance of three thousand yen to support their mother and tubercular brother. Later, she had begun an affair with a man who was helping her to open a small restaurant of her own. After his wife passed away, although Hatsu's sister couldn't become his legal wife, her position nevertheless became more comfortable. That being the case, and since the sister could no longer bear children herself, she had hit upon the idea of doing all she could to get Hatsu married and then adopting one of the resulting children. Conveniently, just then she had happened to notice a man who came into her shop to drink, whose wife had passed away leaving him with two children, and who was looking to remarry. So, after discussing matters with him, she sent a letter to Hatsu, saying, *Why don't you ask for some time off and come to Wakayama? The man is someone I've known for a while, so you can be confident about him, and I feel certain the matter will go well.*

With two prospects coming at the same time, Hatsu was at a loss. As far as Raikichi and the rest of the family were concerned, it was hard to imagine sending this girl—though she was hardly a girl any longer—who had lived under their roof for nearly twenty years off to be married in some strange place. It would be a different question if she were returning to her hometown in Kagoshima, but the man in question lived in Wakayama, a place Hatsu had never even visited! They had met Hatsu's sister once when she visited Kyoto with her patron, so they knew her character, but as for the man who proposed to take Hatsu as his bride, well, surely the sister couldn't be terribly mistaken in anything she had said about him, but was it safe to trust her so completely? The man lived in a farmhouse outside of Wakayama City and said that Hatsu, having grown up in a farming and fishing family, would be an enormous help, but it had been years and years since Hatsu had lived in the countryside and worked in the fields, and she had gotten used to life in Kyoto. Could she really be satisfied with a rural life once she'd had a taste of the big city? After a while, wouldn't she begin to find fault with everything there? Could a woman who had lived among fine things and learned delicate manners really go right back to being a provincial again? It was too pathetic! Even now, Raikichi and Sanko sometimes would recall the time that Hatsu had gone home for two or three months to work on the farm and had come back to them deeply tanned from working in the fields; no, the very thought of such a fate was unbearable. And that was to say nothing of the man's two children by his former wife. How would Hatsu get along with them?—that was a whole other question.

About the pharmacy owner, on the other hand, they couldn't know much until they investigated, but at least he had no children, so there was nothing to worry about on that score. She could be married from the Shimogamo house, with the Chikuras standing in for her parents. And if, after trying it, she didn't like married life, she could leave him; Raikichi and the others would always welcome her back. Of course they weren't hoping for such an outcome!

But these were the thoughts of the Shimogamo house. In the final analysis, Raikichi and Sanko may have been thinking too much of their own convenience. As for Hatsu, now that their mother back home had passed away, she thought of her older sister as a sort of second mother and couldn't easily reject her advice. If she were going to leave the Chikura household, her home was no longer in Kagoshima, but in Wakayama. She recognized the debt she owed to the Chikura family, but her older sister was the only person she could rely upon in the end. While she repeatedly told Raikichi, Sanko, Nioko, Numeko, and Mutsuko that she hated to leave them—*Even when I go to Wakayama, it's not certain that the marriage negotiations will go smoothly, so for now I'll help my sister out at the restaurant, and though Kagoshima is far away, Wakayama is no distance at all, so I'll happily visit any time, and if ever I can be of any use to you, I'll rush right over*—and though she sobbed as she cuddled little Miyuki, whom she had cared for as her own daughter, nevertheless she left at the end of that summer, after only four or five months working for Numeko. Miyuki was still at an age when she didn't know East from West, and says now that she doesn't even remember what Hatsu looked like.

Hatsu was soon married just as her sister had planned. Raikichi and his wife didn't attend the ceremony, but it seems that their fears were unfounded and that the couple got along, so it was just as well, they thought, that they hadn't meddled too much. Hatsu now has four children, including the husband's daughters by his first wife, and she's toiling away at the farm work with their help.

Sada was the first of the Chikura maids to be joined in marriage with someone she met through the offices of Raikichi and his wife. I mentioned her earlier, while telling Koma's story. She was from northern Kawachi, in Osaka prefecture, and came to the Chikura household one or two months after Koma, but this was not her first experience in service. In her previous position, she had ingratiated herself to the family of a famous kyōgen actor of the Ōkura school, Haruyama Sengorō, and gained that man's confidence to such a degree that he told her he hoped she would marry his son. And she worked very hard after she came to the Chikura house. Right around that time, Raikichi was making some alterations to the pavilion he used as his study, the "Gōkantei," and three or four carpenters and craftsmen were staying at the house, so Sada took care of all their meals, waking up at five to prepare breakfast no matter how late she'd gone to bed the night before. She never uttered a word of complaint about the work. In addition, she loved children, and she was particularly tenderhearted toward animals, carefully looking after the family's cat and dogs. A maid who understands animals is so desirable in a household that keeps pets, and yet quite difficult to find! Occasionally one finds a maid who loves dogs, but almost all of them hate cats. If you're not careful, cats can get into the Japanese-style rooms and soil clothes and floor cushions, and they steal sashimi or grilled fish if you don't keep an eye on them, and that means more laundry and scoldings from the master; and if, in secret, you punish the cat, it will report back to the cat-loving master, and soon he knows all about it. At the Shimogamo house at this time there was, in addition to the two spitz dogs, a female Japanese cat named "Mii," and since every single member of the family—Raikichi and his wife, Nioko, Numeko, and Mutsuko—all adored the cat, they were fortunate to find a maid like Sada who would show it affection.

Sada's unusual love for children and animals was thought to have something to do with her unhappy childhood. Her father, a school-master in Hokkaido, had two daughters—Sada and her older sis-ter—but when, for some reason, he separated from his wife, the two girls were sent to live with her family, and that's when Sada's troubles began. The wife came from a rather wealthy farming family, but Sada was sent at the age of fourteen to live with childless relatives. When her foster parents gave birth to a son of their own soon after, Sada's position in the house plunged from daughter to nursemaid for the boy, and her life became a succession of bitter and difficult days. She at least was permitted to attend the public middle school, though. Her older sister was less fortunate: she was sent to live with another family at the age of twelve and was not allowed to finish even ele-mentary school; then, when she reached marriageable age, she was deceived by a bad man who left her with two children, until finally, it's said, she became a Christian. Their birth mother had remarried, so Sada felt she had no choice but to go live with the father who had thrown their mother out of the house, but he too had remarried. In the course of all this, Sada had grown accustomed to waking and beginning her work while it was still dark outside, so she thought it natural to do the same when she went into service in a stranger's house. From childhood, there had never been a single person to pity her or show her compassion, and the lonely girl looked to mute an-imals for friendship, she said.

She sympathized with others' misfortune and did not mind working on their behalf without giving a thought about her own well-being. Happily, she was blessed with an unusually strong constitution and could endure harder work than an ordinary person. That's what had caught the attention of the family of Haruyama Sengorō of the Ōkura school, and it wasn't long before, at Atami too, someone came to admire her work ethic and told the family, *I could find a really fine match for a girl like that, so please leave it to me!* This prospective matchmaker was the owner of the Tomoeya, a grocery store he had built on the road along the coast, with a successful café on the second floor. The Tomoeya supplied the Yamamoto Ryōkan, a large old inn well known in the area. The son of the inn's manager, still just a young man, had gone to Zushi, in Kanagawa prefecture, to live with his elder sister's family and to help out at their catering business, but he wanted to find a suitable wife as soon as possible and become independent; how would Sada feel about moving there? The older sister was quite an industrious sort, and her catering business was flourishing; her husband was the son of the head of the local fishermen's union. If the young man decided to become financially independent of them, he could rely on both the sister's family and his father for the capital to set himself up; he was thinking of staying in the area and opening a sushi shop, so as not to compete with his sister. For that plan to work, he would absolutely a wife no less industrious than his sister, and Miss Sada would be ideal, the master of the Tomoeya said; she was just the sort of person this young man had been searching for.

The arrangements, begun immediately, proceeded without a hitch, and the marriage of Sada and the young man was completed the year after Hatsu went to Wakayama—that must have been the winter of 1954. For the reasons I mentioned above, Sada didn't have a home from which to be married; she had her father, but she wasn't listed in his family register, and she had no mother in the household where she was listed. So the Chikuras stood in for her parents, and the master of the Tomoeya and his wife acted as go-betweens. The ceremony was held in an eight-mat Japanese-style room at the back of the catering shop. Raikichi didn't attend, but Sanko and Mutsuko were there, and they brought Koma along to help out. Those three were the only guests on the bride's side. On the groom's side, in addition to the elder sister and her husband, there were a few groups of people who seemed to be relatives or friends—fewer than fifteen, altogether. The reception was held in the same eight-mat room, but it was too small even for so few guests, so they spread some blankets in the hallway for the overflow. The ceremony was very simple, with no offering for the priest, nor the usual boy and girl hired to pour out *sake* for ceremonial toasts—the elder sister's young daughter served in that role instead. The newlyweds left that evening on their honeymoon to Mine hot springs, Sanko and the others taking the same train as far as Atami. The newlyweds spent one night at the hot spring and then returned, stopping in Atami to express their thanks and bearing traditional dolls and other gifts for Sada's old comrades; Raikichi remembers the new husband and wife in the garden, playing around with a new camera, snapping picture after picture.

About nine years have passed since then. The sushi shop has flourished—they now employ fifty or sixty people. And they have three children. The husband works hard, and, with such a resourceful wife, I'm sure they've saved quite a tidy sum. Up to this point, at least, Sada is perhaps the most successful of all the maids who worked for the Chikura household.

I believe there were more than a few maids who made matches and got married after Sada's wedding, but none of them were in service very long, and each of them returned to her hometown to be married from her parents' house, so Raikichi and the others don't know much about their present circumstances. Occasionally one will send a New Year's card, so we hear that she's become a good housewife, but we have no news about most of them. There were two after Sada, though, who made impressive marriages and held splendid ceremonies at which Raikichi and Sanko stood in for their parents: those two beauties, Gin and Suzu.

While Sada's wedding had been quite a forlorn affair, even Raikichi attended these two. The owner of a deluxe inn at Izusan served as go-between for Suzu and her eventual husband, and in Gin's case her grandmother and mother traveled together from Kagoshima and invited the neighbors in for a brilliant display of the wedding gifts. What's more, the two of them held their weddings on the same day at the same place — the Izusan Gongen Shrine. First Suzu and her groom exchanged vows, then Gin and hers. Gin's reception was held at the home of a relative who lives by the steps leading to the shrine, while Suzu's was at the shrine annex, and Raikichi gave speeches at both venues congratulating the couples. But these two wedding ceremonies were held three or four years after Sada's, and in that time all sorts of things happened, particularly concerning Gin, so I should really get all that down. I've already mentioned that it took a few years for Gin to develop the sort of looks that really attract attention; but she was already capturing hearts early on, when she first came to Shimogamo at the age of nineteen. One of these was a young man who worked at a dry cleaners called Hakuhaku-sha. He pursued her zealously — probably because of that face like the famous actress's, more than anything else. In those days, though, Gin was still an innocent child and had no thought of such things. She didn't even notice the dry-cleaning boy's advances. She used to go about her chores blithely singing that song, "Because the moon is so blue."

Chapter Fourteen

ALTHOUGH IT'S RATHER COMPLICATED, I'D LIKE TO
add a note here reviewing the various addresses of the Chikura
household, which moved several times after the war.

In 1946, Raikichi and his wife left behind the rural village in
Okayama prefecture to which they had been deployed and rented
rooms in Kyoto, in the northern part of the city, near the intersection
of Teramachi and Imadegawa avenues. Almost immediately, however, they set up a house in the eastern part of the city, in Nanzenji
Shimokawaracho, alongside the flowing Shirakawa river. Before
long, they transferred that house to Asukai Jirō and his wife and
moved to the estate in the sacred grove at Shimogamo Shrine, with
its ponds and waterfall and landscaped hills, its lovely groves and
springs. While they were still living at the aforementioned Nanzenji,
they once again established a second home in Atami, first renting a
villa on the grounds of the Sannō Hotel from a friend and then, after
moving the main house to Shimogamo, buying a villa in Atami, in
the Nakada neighborhood. It was during the Nakada period that

Ume's epileptic seizures, the Great Fire of 1950, and Sayo's lesbian affair all occurred.

In around 1955, a bus began running out to Nakada, and as the number of inns and geisha houses increased, the area around their home was transformed into a pleasure quarter—an inhospitable environment for Raikichi and the others—so they sold that villa and moved up the mountainside to Narusawa in Izusan, just about halfway between Atami Station and Yugawara Station, where they live to this day. Sada's wedding dates to this period in Narusawa.

Narusawa is within the Atami city limits, but until six or seven years ago the atmosphere there was still quite tranquil. It's not even a two-and-a-half-mile walk from the station, and in those days you could stroll back and forth, watching the bay expectantly for plumes of smoke from the volcanic island of Ōshima. The novelist Mr. Kiga and his wife, who now live in the Tokiwamatsu area of Shibuya, in Tokyo, were then living less than a mile to the east, in Ōboradai. The artist Yokoyama Taikan had a villa in the neighborhood, too. Raikichi's family gave their mountain villa the name Shōheki Cottage, a reference to the Yangtze river. It faced a long path of stone steps leading to the statue of the Kōa Kannon erected by the former general of the Imperial Army, Matsui Iwane,* and the sound of the great drum—struck by the temple-keeper, apparently a follower of the Tendai sect—echoed across to them every morning and evening without fail, no matter how hot or cold the day. Atami is known as a winter resort, and the veranda of the villa in Narusawa was warm and sunny even in the coldest months and surprisingly cool in the summer, since it was in the mountains. If you took a car there, you had to get out at the foot of the path and climb laboriously up about

---

* The "Raising-Asia" statue of the bodhisattva of mercy was built by Matsui to honor those who died in battle in the Second Sino-Japanese War, both Japanese and Chinese. Matsui was convicted of war crimes and executed for his role in the Nanjing Massacre, and in 1948 his ashes were interred at the temple along with those of six other war criminals.—Tr.

sixty steps. Was it difficult? Of course, but not much of an agony once you got used to it.

Raikichi and the family spent two or three years in this way, going back and forth between Atami in the summer and winter and Kyoto in the spring and fall, but it gradually became a nuisance, and since Atami, being so close to Tokyo, was in many ways more convenient, at last they made the Narusawa villa their base of operations and completely pulled out of the Shimogamo house in Kyoto, to which they had grown so accustomed. That was at the end of 1956. Of course, the Shimogamo house is gone now, but they still have the Asukai house near Shirakawa, in Kyoto, and Keisuke and his wife Numeko live there. Nioko generally stays with her older sister at the Narusawa house, but even she goes off to Kyoto several times a year. Raikichi and Sanko feel an attachment to that city, so they use the Asukai house as their vacation home, sleeping in a room on the second floor and staying, sometimes, as long as ten days or two weeks, until they feel they're becoming a burden.

Shōheki Cottage wasn't as spacious as the old Shimogamo estate. The Shimogamo house was set on a plot of seven hundred *tsubo*, or over half an acre, while the cottage was on a plot of not even two hundred *tsubo*, and the house itself was only about eighty *tsubo*. Happily, though, there was a vacant lot next door, completely covered with thickly grown reeds and pampas grass. Who knew what the owner was thinking, leaving a lot vacant like that in such a prime location, but he told Raikichi, "I don't want to sell, but you may use it if you like—just don't build anything on it. Anyway, it's vacant, so I don't mind if you want to get some exercise there. I won't charge you rent for that. And if I ever do decide to sell, I'll talk to you first." Accepting the owner's generous offer, Raikichi began to clear some of the reeds and pampas grass, and then he laid down sod to make a winding path through the space. Faithful to their agreement, he refrained from any real building on the lot, but he had three double weeping cherry trees brought from Kyoto—just like the ones at the Heian Shrine — and planted several Yoshino cherry trees around them. He also set up an arbor for wisteria in the northeast corner. He asked for a division of a crinum lily from the Kiga house and planted a clump of bush-clover and so on, and next he built a simple gazebo and a dog house — the sort of things that could be easily dismantled if necessary. Raikichi and the others called this space the "back garden." In addition to the stone steps out front that led up to the Kōa Kannon, there was a stairway from this back garden descending to the street below in just fifty steps, and sometimes people wanting to pay their respects to the Kannon would take this other path by mistake and wander into the back garden. These same steps would later play a significant role in Gin's love affair.

Raikichi and his wife, together with Nioko and Mutsuko, often headed over to Atami for some entertainment. A broad avenue runs in a straight line from the beach toward Nishiyama, the most bustling street in town — when did it come to be called "Atami Ginza"? I feel as though it can't have been that long ago. When Raikichi and the others wanted to shop, or see a movie, or kill time in a café or sushi shop, there was no other option but to head there. At least once a day someone from the family called a Shōnan taxi. Actually, the family often called a taxi two or three times in a day, so I suppose the taxi company had no customers more loyal. This taxi company was about half a mile from Narusawa toward Atami Station, four or five houses down from the foot of the Aizomebashi bridge; when called, they would come to the foot of the stone steps within seven or eight minutes. There must have been about twenty-five drivers, and it goes without saying that all of them were acquainted with the Chikura family. The maids ordinarily took the bus when they went into town, but sometimes they got a ride back home in an empty cab headed that way after dropping someone off. No other favor was more appreciated by maids carrying heavy packages of vegetables, fish, and fruit. They would get out of the cab at Aizomebashi and change to the bus, but it depended on the driver; some would take a maid past the bridge all the way to Narusawa and let them off at the foot of the stone steps.

It was one of these taxis that brought Gin and Mitsuo together. Mitsuo, the only son of an elderly couple who ran a modest restaurant in Yugawara, had been working as a driver for Shōnan Taxi for about ten years. Mitsuo's parents were natives of Izusan, and had run a reasonably successful catering business there in the past, only moving out of the city toward Yuguwara as business had declined, so it wasn't as though their son, Mitsuo, was some carpetbagger about whom nothing was known. But as far as Raikichi could see, he was the commonest sort of boy from town, and could hardly be considered handsome enough for someone as special as Gin. He lacked the sort of good looks that would distinguish him from the other twenty-four drivers, and yet there was something about him that appealed to the young women in the neighborhood. He was quite popular among the maids at the local inns; indeed, so great was his reputation that, when calling for a taxi, they would frequently specify, "Send Mitsuo-san." When exactly the romance between them had begun, not even Gin could say for certain. Perhaps it was on her way home from shopping in what is still called the "Atami Ginza"; or, whenever Sanko or Nioko headed off to Tokyo or Kyoto, someone would always go to see them off from the train platform, so perhaps it was returning from such a trip to the station, or on some other random occasion, but what is certain is that Gin often received a ride home from Mitsuo in his taxi. And, from early on, she noticed that he would cast flirting glances at her reflection in the rearview mirror. It was then that she began to pay attention to the young man named Mitsuo.

One day, Nioko announced that she would go to Kyoto, and Gin accompanied her to the station. The driver of the taxi they took there was Mitsuo. When she had seen her mistress off, Gin left the platform and exited the ticket gate to find Mitsuo's taxi still waiting. When she asked, "What are you doing?" he replied:

"I'm waiting for you. I'll take you back home. Get in."

Mitsuo had an unusually rough, almost bullying way of speaking. According to the local girls, there was something fascinating in that bullying tone.

"I'm staying in town," Gin said. "I have some shopping to do."

"Then I'll take you that way. Come on, get in. It won't take long, right?"

"I have a lot of errands to do. I have to stop at five or six places. And I have to go the post office and send off a lot of registered mail. It's bound to take some time."

"Oh well. I'll see you later then."

"All right. Oh, wait —" Gin took out the two hundred-yen bills Nioko had given her for the taxi. "Here."

"I don't need that."

"I'll be in trouble if you don't take it. My mistress gave it to me to pay for the taxi ride."

"Didn't I say I don't need it? Keep it for pocket money."

"I really don't feel right …"

"I said take it, okay? Right, see you." As he returned the two hundred-yen bills, Mitsuo pressed the palm of Gin's hand forcefully.

And then, there was this incident:

Sanko went to visit the home of the painter Yamahata Katsushirō and, once again, Gin accompanied her. The Yamahata estate is in a remote, untraveled spot; to get there, you drive under the pedestrian overpass in front of the station and then climb several hundred yards up Momoyama, going around and around on the mountain road, and then turn left. Here, too, there is a set of steep stone steps up to the entrance to the house, so Sanko got out at the foot of the steps and climbed up. She usually spent one or two hours there, chatting with the painter and his wife, so she would send the taxi away and have the driver take her maid back to the house. Well, on this day, Gin accompanied Sanko as far as the glass door of the entrance and then descended the stone steps to get into the waiting car, when all of a sudden Mitsuo grabbed her from behind and kissed her! It was an elaborate kiss, filled with passion, and it left Gin speechless and compliant. After several such episodes, Gin's feelings toward Mitsuo changed dramatically. Something was boiling up in the heart of this girl from the south, something pure and heedless, like an uncontrollable torrent that flowed where it would, and suddenly she could not live another moment without Mitsuo. Raikichi and the others didn't notice, but now, whenever a taxi was called to the house, it was invariably Mitsuo's that arrived. This was because Gin insisted on making the phone call and asked them to be sure to send Mitsuo if he was free. Those other maids who knew the situation, though they were shocked at her infatuation, kept Gin's secret from the master and his wife and summoned Mitsuo as often as possible too. So Mitsuo would approach along the national highway that runs below the house, honking his horn to signal his arrival, park the car at the foot of the stone steps, and as was his habit, sing the first line of Mihashi Michiya's song, "From Apple Village": "Do you remember the town of your birth?"

Gin didn't always accompany the master when he took a cab, but still she would come flying down the stairs ahead of him to take her boyfriend's hand and then see them off with obvious affection, waving as she watched the taxi drive off into the distance, dipping in and out of sight as it descended the road to Narusawa and then traveled along the national highway toward Atami, hugging the shore, turn after turn.

At the foot of those stone steps to Shōheki Cottage, just where the taxis parked and waited, stood the villa of Tamai Ryōhei, the president of Kotani Manufacturing. He and his wife would sometimes jaunt down from Tokyo in their Benz and stay over Saturday and Sunday to play golf at the Kawana course or whatnot, but usually the only people there were a widowed maid of forty-five or so named O-yone, who looked after the house, and the two children, who attended the local elementary school. A detached caretaker's cottage had been built near the front gate to the villa, with a rustic twig gate in front, and at some point O-yone got used to seeing Mitsuo's car outside and hearing the song, "From Apple Village." Sometimes, whether she wanted to or not, she was forced to witness scenes of Gin running down to meet Mitsuo and then holding his hand or kissing him. Needless to say, such scenes only gained in passion in the shadows of dusk. Even in the bright light of midday, those two didn't care if someone saw them. They would get into the car together and start grappling, until O-yone ran away in a panic.

There was another reason why Gin watched Mitsuo's car regretfully as it drove off, and kept watching until it was out of sight. Along the highway he took back to town, between Narusawa and Aizomebashi, was an inn called the Shōtōkan, or "Rippling Pines Inn," and a maid there named Kane was partial to Mitsuo. Kane knew about Gin and Mitsuo, and would wait for his car and blow him a kiss or give him a wink as he passed, or, if she had time, get him to pick her up and take her for a drive. This made Gin burn with unbearable jealousy. After Mitsuo's empty cab departed, Gin would strain her ears to determine whether he stopped the car at the Shōtōkan or not. If she grew suspicious, she would run down to the end of the stone stairs and back, and she couldn't relax until she knew whether he had stopped. Often, if Raikichi was away, she would run to his study and stand at the south-facing window with a view of Hatsushima and Ōshima, because from there one could follow the path of Mitsuo's taxi for quite a long way, and it would be impossible for him to conceal it if he loitered in front of the Shōtōkan.

Mitsuo's appeal was not limited to that maid, though. It was said he was on intimate terms with one of the woman bus conductors, for instance, and that he was hopelessly popular among the maids in Atami, so if Gin obsessed over each of them, there would be no end to her jealousy. It was even said that once, when he was giving one woman a ride and was stopped by another, he said, "Why don't you get in?" and shoved the first woman into the rumble seat!

When Suzu was going into town to do some shopping on the master's orders, Gin would often tell her, "Suzu-san, call for Mitsuo to take you," and give her money for the fare. For Gin, this meant that she knew Mitsuo's whereabouts and could rest easy that he wasn't stealing a chance to go cruising downtown. For Suzu, on the other hand, being treated to a taxi ride was a big help with her heavy packages, so she certainly didn't complain.

Chapter Fifteen

TRAINS COMING FROM TOKYO ON THE NATIONAL
Rail line entered a tunnel right after leaving Yugawara Station. It was
rather a long tunnel, and the trains emerged at the Izusan hot springs,
just past an inn called "Torikyō," or "Peach and Plum Border," then
quickly entered a second and a third tunnel, coming out beyond Aizomebashi. The first tunnel ends just a short distance from Shōheki
Cottage, midway between the Narusawa and Oku-Narusawa bus
stops, where the bus turns slightly from the national road toward
the coast. Gin would sometimes climb up to a place right above the
mouth of the tunnel, squat above it, and spend hours looking down
at the passing trains and crying. At such times, you could be certain
that she had quarreled with Mitsuo—perhaps because someone had
seen him in town giving a ride to a woman from somewhere or other,
or because Gin had gotten a harassing phone call from the woman
bus conductor, or he had stood her up—but always something tri-
fling that nevertheless upset her terribly.

Crying out "I can't stand it!" or "I wish I could die!" she would drop whatever she was doing and run out of the kitchen. When Koma or Suzu ran after her in concern, they would find that she had dashed down the stone stairs and disappeared in the direction of the train tracks. "Gin-san! Gin-san! Where are you going?" they would shout, but Gin wouldn't even look back. If they followed her, they would find Gin squatting over that tunnel, deep in thought. "What are you doing in a place like this? You'll get us all in trouble, you know."

Finally, even her friends got so used to Gin shouting about dying that it no longer surprised them much. When she started it up again, they would shout "Gin-san! Gin-san!" and run after her as before, but now they would give up the chase midway and return to the house. Sure enough, Gin would turn up two or three hours later but, seeing the faces of her friends, she would be plunged into depression again. At such times, she would call the taxi company incessantly and insist on seeing Mitsuo's face that day, no matter what. She would call persistently, as late as two or three in the morning, wrapping the bell of the telephone with a piece of paper or a cloth to muffle its ringing, just as Hatsu and the others had done in the past. Her friends, exhausted by the drama, had long since retreated to the maids' room and gone to bed, but Gin wouldn't leave off. Giving in at last, Mitsuo would wake up, rub the sleep from his eyes, and resign himself to walking over, nearly a mile through the dark. Gin, lying in wait on the stone steps, would seize him there, and a violent lovers' quarrel would ensue. Not only did Mitsuo have a rough way of speaking, but he also had a bit of a lisp and couldn't speak very smoothly or fluently, so when they got into it, he tended to fight with his hands rather than words. Soon it devolved into a brawl, the two of them punching and kicking and scratching. Of course, Gin wasn't the only one prey to jealousy. Before she became involved with Mitsuo, she had been close with someone who worked for Shōwa Taxi in Atami. She hadn't dated him long at all and had cut it off completely, but Mitsuo knew about it, and when

Gin's jealous rants became too harsh, he would respond by throwing that in her face, and the brawl would escalate.

The Chikura villa stood on the right-hand side of the stone steps that led up to the Kōa Kannon; on the left-hand side, directly opposite, stood a much grander villa. This recently became the property of the singer Segawa Michio, and I understand he goes there sometimes to relax, but it used to belong to the president of a certain private railway, or so people said, and it stood empty just about year-round—Raikichi and the others had never even seen the shutters opened. There was a strip of lawn in front of the main part of the house, and a single large camphor tree, visible from the porch of our villa, towered over it, extending its thick branches. Well, this empty villa and its garden provided the perfect rendezvous spot for Gin and Mitsuo. When they wanted to have an unhurried talk, they would slip away there to spend some time together. They could meet in the garden of the empty villa in the evening, of course, and even in broad daylight without anyone questioning them. They could embrace there—or fight, or flirt—to their hearts' content.

Once, one of her friends picked up a scrap of a letter that Gin had written and then torn up and thrown away. Glancing at it casually, she saw that it was addressed to Gin's grandmother back in her home-town and said, "I truly am in need, so please send me three hundred thousand yen." All the maids wondered why Gin would need such a lot of money; well, she was worried about debts Mitsuo had incurred by living beyond his means. The thing is, he had fallen in with some unsavory types and gotten into the habit of going out to gamble with them. They were all professionals at that sort of thing, so he had no chance of winning when he gambled against them. Sometimes they would let him win, but in general, he went home the loser. His debts piled up, and the more desperate he became to win back the money, the more he invited the opposite result until, before he knew it, he had incurred debts of over six or seven hundred thousand yen. Needless to

124

say, Gin tearfully implored him to do something to extricate himself from this band of gamblers. The three hundred thousand yen she had asked her grandmother for was meant to be applied to these debts, to help lift him from this quagmire, but her grandmother wasn't likely to send such an amount without knowing the reason.

At one point, Mitsuo suddenly said, "What am I gonna do? Isn't there any way to get fifty thousand yen by today?"

"Fifty thousand yen? What for?"

"If I don't get the money, something terrible will happen—"

"Something terrible?!"

"They're gonna 'trim my hand.'"

"Trim your hand? What do you mean?"

"They're gonna cut off my finger."

"Does it have to be the whole fifty thousand?"

"I have to keep my promise. Those type are really strict about rules. Once you make a promise, you have to keep it. And if you don't pay back your debts, you lose a finger—anyone who falls in with those guys has to be ready for that."

"But why did you fall in with such men?"

"What's the use of asking that now?!"

"When do you need the money by?"

"Today."

"Can't you ask them to wait a few days?"

"There's no way they'll wait. They made that clear from the start."

I mentioned above that Gin's family back in Kagoshima was rather well off. Just after she joined the Chikura household, her salary was three thousand yen a month, but later she was getting three thousand five hundred. In addition to that, she received about one or two thousand each month from her grandmother for pocket money, and more if she asked. She should have been better off financially than any of her friends, but she was lavishing most of her money on Mitsuo. First of all, the taxi fares she paid every day amounted to quite a sum. When he was in a good mood, Mitsuo would refuse money for the fare, saying, "I don't need it," but after one of their lovers' quarrels, he would take the money without a word. Beyond what she paid him directly, the money Gin gave her friends to treat themselves to rides in Mitsuo's taxi added up to a not insignificant amount. Mitsuo liked beer, so sometimes she would come down the stone steps to meet him with a bottle. When she knew what time to expect him, she would discreetly chill the bottle of beer in the icebox in advance. She also bought him fancy neckties at a store in town that sells western goods. Between this and that, she didn't have a cent left in her savings account these days. So she was in no way capable of raising fifty thousand yen.

"Couldn't you borrow it from someone else?"

"I've got no way out. Can't you do something?"

"I don't know what to tell you …"

Gin thought for a moment, then had an idea.

"I don't know if she can help, but anyway, let's talk to Suzu-san."

"Does Suzu-san have that kind of money?"

"Mitsuo-san, if you borrow that money from her, do you intend to pay her back?"

"I'll pay it back. If I can't pay it all back at one time, then I'll split it into two payments. If you give me just two months, I can pay it all back."

"You really will pay it all back, right? You promise? If you don't, I'll be in a fix."

This was Gin's plan. At the turnoff from the national road heading up to Shōheki Cottage stood an inn called "Shōgetsurō," or Shining Moon Mansion. The head clerk there—the maids all called him "The Receptionist"—was a young man named Hasegawa Seizō. Gin knew that Suzu was on intimate terms with this young man, and she suspected that he had some money saved. So, as a last resort, she thought she would get Suzu to ask Hasegawa for the money.

"Sure, I'll ask him. I think he'll probably agree." Suzu left immediately, and, a short while later, returned with five ten-thousand-yen
bills.

"Thank you! Thank you! This will save Mitsuo's finger! I'll never
forget this!"

"Never mind that; just tell Mitsuo to cut his ties to those gamblers. Until he does, you mustn't get engaged to him."

Later, that same Hasegawa married Suzu; perhaps this incident
brought them closer.

Now then, at this point, another young woman, a formidable rival
of Gin's, is ushered onto our stage.

The young woman's name was Yuri, or "Lily." Yuri entered service
with the Chikura household around the same time as Gin, but a few
months earlier, when the Shimogamo house was still the family's
principal residence. If she hasn't appeared in this story until now,
that's because she didn't work for the family steadily, but left and
returned repeatedly without ever settling in. To be quite honest, this
girl was Raikichi's favorite; in some ways, he liked her even better
than Gin or Suzu. At one time, while they were living in Kyoto, he
enjoyed nothing more than to go walking around the Kawaramachi
area or to see a movie with her, to the point that he wouldn't ask anyone else to join him. And yet, she wasn't a beauty like Gin or Suzu.
She was a year younger than Suzu, so she must have been a year older
than Gin. Small of frame and a bit shorter than those two, she had
a round, flat face—a face like a plate, as they say—as she herself acknowledged. However, her skin was very fair, and she was pleasantly
plump; her arms and legs weren't unattractive; her feet were as pretty
as a child's; and about her whole body there was a voluptuousness.
Come to think of it, there was one distinctive feature to Yuri's face.
Just next to her right eye, only a hair away, was a tiny little mole. It
was so small that it didn't look like a mole at all, and many people
mistook it for a bit of snot. Raikichi himself made this mistake once.

"Hey," he said, "you've got something just there," and tried to brush it off.

Raikichi liked walking with her more than anyone else because she was so lively and cheerful, and so unreserved around her master. The other girls—even a veteran like Hatsu or someone as confident as Suzu—maintained a slight formality when they went out alone with Raikichi. They would respond without hesitation if he spoke to them, but they wouldn't initiate conversation themselves. And if Raikichi said something funny, they wouldn't laugh out loud; if they laughed at all, it was only delicately. If Yuri had something interesting to say, though, she would freely bring it up herself. Sometimes she would even banter with Raikichi or tease him, and she never bored him. Thinking that it might help to keep him young, Sanko once suggested to Raikichi that he find a young geisha in the Gion quarter to dote on, but when he tried this, Raikichi found he couldn't be bothered with all the trouble he had to take with such a girl, and said that he found it much more invigorating to spend time with Yuri.

Since she became Raikichi's constant companion, it goes without saying that Yuri was a perceptive and clever girl, quick to read people. Being such a girl, she also had an independent streak; she could be temperamental, opinionated, and arrogant; and she often clashed with Raikichi. She could be terribly kind and good-humored when so inclined, but when she grew disagreeable, she'd fall into a sulk and take on an indescribably gloomy aspect. Sanko was constantly taking offense at such behavior, and Yuri's reputation among the other maids was abysmal. She took advantage of the fact that she was Raikichi's favorite to intimidate the others and she pushed around the younger maids. Even Suzu, who was only a few months her junior, became the target of her bullying. To make matters worse, quite unlike Sada, she absolutely hated animals. Of course, some of the other servants disliked dogs and cats, but with Yuri, it wasn't a simple dislike; she positively persecuted them. If a cat came near her, she would kick or push it away, crying "Beast!"

More than a few times, one heard from the maids' room someone saying, "I'm taking a break. I just can't deal with it when Yuri's
around!"

"Yuri, please leave this house." One day, Raikichi unexpectedly
handed down his judgment. "You're really very bright. When you
watch a movie, you understand the key points; your penmanship
is good; you understand dressmaking and can sew just about anything quickly and skillfully; you're actually a very valuable person to
have around. The problem is, you can't get along with anyone in the
house. I would give anything to keep you here, but, unfortunately, I
have no alternative but to ask you to leave. If you mend your ways, I
will be happy to have you back at any time."

At that, Yuri did not protest, *I'll reform, only let me stay*! But
rather, saying "Fine, I'll leave," she got her things together and left
immediately.

And this must have happened two or three times. Each time she
returned to the household, it was never on her own initiative, but
because Raikichi, unable to stand her absence, sent her a letter saying
"It was wrong of me to send you away." Even then, Yuri wouldn't listen to his request at first, but would make him ask repeatedly before
at last she deigned to return.

Chapter Sixteen

I'VE SAID THAT YURI HAD A FACE LIKE A PLATE; well, there was another undeniable quality to it. One often encounters that sort of round, flat face in the "low city" of Tokyo, around the Honjo-Fukugawa neighborhood, but there's something different about the same sort of face on a girl who was born and raised in Osaka. Compared with its Edo counterpart, the Osaka face is more evocative of southern climes—more optimistic and cheerful. Raikichi had been raised in Tokyo but, as far as women were concerned, he preferred Osaka, perhaps because his wife Sanko's family were all purebred Osakans. The person who had recommended Yuri to them was Sanko's cousin, also an Osaka woman. When she brought Yuri over to the house, she said to Sanko, "I'm sure you'll like this girl; she's from Osaka," and one look at that face confirmed it.

Indeed, Sanko was absolutely delighted with her—at that moment. "Osaka girls really are the best," she said. "They have such a velvety complexion—quite different from country girls."

Yuri was born near a place called Himejima, in the Nishi-Yodogawa ward of Osaka city, west of Shin-Yodagawa Station and near the border with Hyogo prefecture. Her father had apparently sold fish there, but the business hadn't gone well, so he closed it down and moved the whole family to Fukuoka prefecture, in Kyushu, and went to work at a coal mine in Ōmuta city. That was around the start of the war, when Yuri was in the first grade of elementary school, so she spent most of her early life, from childhood to marriageable age, in a Kyushu mining town. I suppose we should admire her for retaining her Osaka character despite that. Yuri was the eldest child, and had a younger brother and two younger sisters. In addition to her parents, she had a grandmother who was in good health and who made Yuri her particular favorite. Yuri's personality today certainly might be attributed in large part to having been spoiled.

This grandmother had worked in the past as the head nurse at a hospital in Nishinomiya, so she ought to have understood better than most women how these things go, but for some reason she doted on the eldest, Yuri, while mistreating her brother and sisters. Yuri was even given different food and clothing. Anything she wanted, this grandmother would buy for her. When the children's mother rebuked the grandmother for this unequal treatment and tried to remedy it, the grandmother would scold her in return, saying "Why are you making Yuri eat such stuff?" or "wear such clothes?" What really impressed Raikichi from the first was that, whenever Yuri wasn't busy, she would pick up a writing brush and practice her calligraphy on a piece of scrap paper or old newsprint, and this too was due to the grandmother, who had hired a calligraphy teacher to come to the house for Yuri's benefit. Most maids don't know how to write calligraphy on a paper scroll, for instance, but Yuri was quite capable, and she had a pretty good idea of how to write the various cursive styles. This was just around the time that Suzu was receiving penmanship lessons from Raikichi, after which she would practice her letters in the maids' room, and Yuri was so shocked by the clumsiness of Suzu's letters that she would joke about it to Raikichi:

"Sensei, what on earth is this that Suzu's written?!"

"What do you mean 'What is this'?"

Yuri burst out laughing. "No matter how you look at it, that's terrible handwriting. If you ever had her take a letter for you and then mailed it out looking like that, how embarrassing it would be for you—and how insulting to the addressee!"

"No one's asking her to take a letter. After all, there's no need as long as you're here."

"Well, okay then."

"You may laugh, but she's trying her best. And just because she's not very skillful yet doesn't mean she won't be. Of course, she'll never be as good as you; you were born with a talent for calligraphy."

After Yuri graduated from middle school, her grandmother had enrolled her in a dressmaking school, where she completed the curriculum. She earned excellent grades at each school, surpassing her classmates. With her neat hand and her knowledge of *kanji* characters, as well as her skill in sewing, she was understandably rather conceited even after she entered service.

Yuri was one of those people with no sense of direction. There was a shop in the Ginza called Keter that sold German goods—when the family went to Tokyo, the maids were often sent there to buy sausage—and Yuri could never find her way there on her own. Yet she hated to ask anyone for directions, so she would get even more lost until finally she would return home without having gotten whatever she'd been sent out for, because she hadn't been able to locate the shop.

There is an inn called Fukuda-ya in Tokyo, with branches in the Toranomon district of the old Shiba Ward and in the Kioichō district of Kōjimachi Ward. Raikichi stayed at one or the other whenever he went to the city. Kioichō was quieter, so he stayed there when he planned to do some writing, and one time he invited Yuri to join him, to take dictation. However, although Yuri knew the Fukuda-ya in To-ranomon, near Shinbashi Station, she had never been to the one in Kioichō, so, after wandering a while, she dropped by the Toranomon branch and asked the way. The head maid there, Nami-san, aware of Yuri's poor sense of direction, explained it very carefully: Catch the streetcar at Akasaka-Mitsuke, get out at Benkei-bashi, then go this way, then that way. Raikichi also gave her detailed directions over the phone. It wasn't very far, and there weren't any tricky turns, and the road ran along the bank of a river, so he was sure she could find it, but though he waited and waited, she didn't arrive. After quite some time had passed, at last she appeared. It turned out that, wandering aim-lessly around the Benkei-bashi intersection carrying a packed trunk, she had been stopped and questioned by a policeman who mistook her for a runaway. At first, she had thought it better not to mention her master, but the policeman seemed to be growing more and more suspicious, so in the end she opened up the trunk to show him its contents and gave him Raikichi's name; then his attitude completely changed, and he kindly accompanied her all the way to the inn.

Raikichi must have spent the next two or three days sitting across a desk from Yuri, giving dictation. He had always thought her charm-ing but not at all beautiful and yet, over those few days, watching her bent over the manuscript, running her pen across the paper, he found the line of her jaw insanely beautiful.

When it came to music, Yuri was rather tone-deaf. She loved to sing, and would attempt various popular songs, but the result was always quite off-key. Now that I think of it, she was a fan of the actor Takahashi Teiji and seemed to be linked with him in some mysterious way; she would often cross paths with him when walking the Ginza and afterward boast, "I met Takahashi Teiji again today!" Once, on the train from Kyoto to Atami, she sat in the same train car as Takahashi; she was absolutely thrilled at the time. Raikichi thought of Yuri whenever he watched a movie with Takahashi in it:

So Yuri prefers this sort of cheerful-looking guy, he would think, and wanted to set her up with just such a man if he could.

Her taste in food was also unusual. Her grandmother would have treated her to all sorts of delicacies, but she hated anything fancy. Incidentally, the maids in the Raikichi household were accustomed to eating well, and enjoyed great variety in their three daily meals. At breakfast, they ate the same miso soup with grated daikon as the family, rice mixed with a little barley, and the pickled radish for which Atami was famous. For lunch, it was a plain omelet made with one or two eggs, some cooked spinach or green beans, and sashimi or some other dish left over from the family's dinner the previous night. Many of the maids liked fried rice, so sometimes they would make that, with old oil that had already been used two or three times to deep-fry tempura for the family. Other than that, they often ate bean sprouts stir-fried with curry powder, or cod roe, or simmered beans, or sliced squid. For dinner, they would often have simmered pork and vegetables, or a sort of soup with a thick broth and dried fish (another Atami specialty), or a stir-fry of sausage and cabbage, or beef-and-potato croquettes, rice curry, pork cutlets, or, maybe once a week, sukiyaki (this was all paid for by the family, needless to say, along with toiletries, any medical expenses, and so on)—anyway, this is sort of thing they ate, but Yuri didn't like such rich food.

Saying that rice at breakfast upset her stomach, she would take toast instead—with Snow brand butter, not margarine—but often, when it was too much trouble for her to cater to her own simple tastes, she would just mix green onion and grated daikon with some soy sauce, pour it on top of rice, and eat that. When Raikichi invited her a few times to a Chinese restaurant in Shiba Tamura-chō, she turned a blind eye to all the other dishes and took only those Chinese pickles—the ones that taste something like Japanese long-pickled radish, so bitter they pucker your mouth—gulping them down with some green tea poured over rice and exclaiming over how delicious they were. She never looked at all happy when they took her to a fancy restaurant in Kyoto or Tokyo. It was a pleasure to take Suzu out to a restaurant, but there was no point in taking Yuri.

She was a devoted reader of the lady's magazines *Standard* and *Morning Star*, and had a complete set of Tanizaki's adaptation of *The Tale of Genji*. Yuri's visits to the outhouse—which the maids called "the villa"—were famous. It was not unusual for her to spend forty minutes there, lost in some book. She behaved arrogantly and willfully but, having said that, she was not lazy. When the mood struck her, she could clean like a madwoman, moving from room to room until every one was spotless. She had a very hot temper. She was every bit as fastidious in her personal habits as Hatsu had been, and her pale skin glowed that much more because of the care she took with her grooming. I think we can say that this was one reason why Raikichi took to her.

She was straightforward in her dealings with men, in keeping with her brisk disposition; there was never anything lovestruck about her. Her rivalry with Gin led to a lot of complications with Mitsuo, or so I heard, but Yuri detested any hint of impropriety, and this may have contributed to her defeat—I'm certain that her relationship with Mitsuo ended without carnal knowledge.

Circumstances must have been dire for her grandmother to have sent such a cherished granddaughter into service, and when Yuri arrived at the Shimogamo house, she had absolutely nothing with her but the clothes on her back. We still talk about how Mutsuko gave her an old skirt that day because her own was soaked through and she didn't have another to change into. By the time she left service with the Chikura house, though, she had more clothes than any of the other maids, and had amassed such a trousseau that she could have married at any moment; she left with I don't know how many trunks and suitcases. It was only natural, since, each time she quit after fighting with the family, she received severance pay above and beyond her salary as well as all sorts of clothes from Sanko, Nioko, Numeko, and Mutsuko: nightgowns, blouses, skirts, sweaters, cardigans, handbags, and little accessories—she accumulated quite a pile. In the meantime, she mastered the art of makeup by mimicking the women she saw in town, so that the girl whom at first we had all pitied looked like a completely different person. She was no longer a girl from a Kyushu mining town but, from any angle, quite the fashionable Osaka lady. She began to exhibit some vanity and, between chores, would visit beauty parlors. Those she could afford weren't good enough for her, and she would stop by the Kanebō service counter at Shijō-Kawaramachi intead. Sanko noticed that sometimes when she passed Yuri in the hall, she caught the fragrance of Guerlain perfume and felt sure that the girl had taken it from her dressing room. Now that Sanko thought about it, Yuri seemed to be using Elizabeth Arden lipstick and cold cream, too, and, sure enough, she was secretly taking it from her mistress's dresser.

As a sequel to Yuri's story, let me take this opportunity to recount her romantic rivalry with Gin, even though it will be taking events out of order.

Doted on as she was by Raikichi, Yuri began to dream big. She declared that she wanted to go to Tokyo; she wanted to go to Tokyo and work for an actress—not just as a maid, but as the actress's companion, accompanying her to the studio and on location. She was depending on Raikichi and Sanko because they had connections to that world. Of course, if she really wanted to do that it might be possible, but she still hadn't adjusted her moody and arrogant attitude; on the contrary, she was even more impertinent than before. At one point the actress Takane Hidako, who was like family to Raikichi, was looking for a companion, and Yuri could hardly express her joy when it seemed that Takane might take her on; but Raikichi and his wife were worried about recommending a girl with so many faults, and couldn't help thinking that it might really go to Yuri's head if she went to work for a top actress like "Dako-chan"—a star among stars. Raikichi also worried that, because of their close connection, Hidako might feel obligated to hire Yuri if he recommended her. On the other hand, how happy it would make Yuri to be recommended to Takane! They longed to see the joy on her face. And now that this ideal position had become available, it seemed unfair to conceal it from her. One day, Sanko visited Hidako and frankly described both Yuri's good points and her defects, and Hidako agreed to hire her.

Yuri began living in the Takane house as maid-companion to Hidako in the summer of 1956, I believe, when she hadn't yet ended things with Mitsuo. Right up until he married Gin, Mitsuo continued to promise Yuri, "I'll never marry that woman. With that scar on her forehead? No way! I'd run from the wedding hall." Perhaps it wasn't complete nonsense; he may have felt that way at first.

Chapter Seventeen

ON THE DAY THAT SANKO TOOK YURI OVER TO DAKO-
chan's house, she felt that the girl looked a bit shabby for an appointment with a famous actress, so they stopped at Takashimaya
department store on the way, and she bought Yuri a more flattering
blouse and had her change in the lady's room. Having entrusted Yuri
to her new employer, Sanko took her leave and, as she said goodbye
to Hidako at the door, she saw Yuri standing behind the actress, her
eyes brimming with tears; it was quite out of character, but apparently obstinate Yuri could be overcome by sentiment after all, and
Sanko was strangely moved to think that such an arrogant girl had
this other side to her.

Dako-chan found Yuri to be quite useful. She could sew up a
simple chemise with ease and could write out notes for her with no
trouble. Most convenient of all, she had a good general knowledge of
cooking, thanks to her training in the Chikura household. Now that
Yuri's long-held dream had come true and she was the companion
to a big star, she could boast to her family and friends and lord it

over her former colleagues. Once filming began, she carried the case holding greasepaint and other cosmetics and rode with Dako-chan in her private car to the studio. She accompanied the star on location, too—even to Hokkaido in the far north and Kyushu in the south. The minor actors traveled to such remote locations by train in a second-class car, but Dako-chan traveled by plane, and as her companion, Yuri had special permission to travel with her, sitting in the next seat. Soon she had flown to every part of Japan, until there was hardly a place she didn't know. When they stayed at a hotel, she went down to the restaurant with the star, sat at the same table with her, and ordered from the same menu. This period was perhaps the zenith of her life. No matter how splendid a marriage she might make in the future, she was unlikely to enjoy such success again.

However, just as Raikichi and the others had feared, Yuri's character emerged little by little, and her true colors were revealed. She insulted the minor actors and spoke to them condescendingly, which was most embarrassing to Hidako. She would use the same tone of voice with them as Hidako did, as though her status was the same as the star's. They all thought she was an impertinent thing but said nothing, out of consideration for Hidako. This put the actress in an intolerable position. People might think that she was allowing Yuri to behave this way, and nothing could be more offensive. Again and again she warned Yuri to mend her ways, but when it came down to it, Yuri would somehow forget those warnings. There were two other servants in the Takane household, an older maid who had been there for a long time and a driver, and Yuri bullied these two as well. She treated the driver particularly harshly, ordering him around as brusquely as though she were his master. He was stoical, though, and took it all without losing his temper.

"I thought it would come to this," Sanko told Dako-chan. "I can't tell you how sorry I am to have caused you so much trouble. If that's the case, please fire her; you needn't worry about offending us, and you certainly don't owe Yuri anything." She said this on several occasions, but Dako-chan, having overcome childhood poverty to reach her present position, was rather softhearted and compassionate to those she employed and found it hard to let them go even if they became an inconvenience.

"It's kind of you to say that, but she has her good points, too," she replied. "And if Yuri-chan leaves, there's no one to take her place." So she continued to employ her, and Yuri thought to herself, "She's helpless without me."

Sometimes when they flew to a location, Yuri's favorite male movie star would travel on the same plane. Yuri would forget her duties as companion and leave her seat next to Hidako to sit beside him. And once, at the Sapporo Grand Hotel, the following incident occurred. As usual, Yuri was directed to the hotel restaurant, where she was seated across from Hidako and shown the dinner menu. Preferring light food as she did, Yuri particularly struggled with western cuisine and fell into a bad mood whenever she was presented with this sort of hotel restaurant menu; on this day she must have been in a bad mood, for she angrily refused to say anything. Even after Hidako ordered, she just sat there, sulking silently.

Hidako gave in and spoke first. "Is something wrong, Yuri-chan? What would you like to eat?"

"I won't have anything."

"Shouldn't you eat something?"

"There's nothing here for me to eat."

"But you'll get hungry later."

"Thanks for your concern. I'll have some sushi or something when I go back to my room."

Everything was in this tone.

Both Raikichi and Sanko had weak constitutions and took several pills each day, so Yuri had become quite knowledgeable about medicine, and she cavalierly advised Hidako to take various pills and supplements herself. She regularly recommended Zett-P after dinner for digestion, Chlortrimeton for a stuffed nose, vitamin B or the multivitamin Guronsan for fatigue, and Adalin, Luminal, or Lavona (phenobarbital) to help her sleep. But Hidako, who had a strong constitution and had never taken any sort of drug regularly, said, "I don't need that; there's nothing wrong with me," and this again annoyed Yuri—she couldn't rest until she had somehow made her mistress take something. At times, contrary to all reason, Hidako would even try to curry favor with Yuri.

There's a breed of dog called a Border Collie. Most people have heard of an ordinary Collie, but you never see a Border Collie—even some pet shop owners don't know the name. This sort of dog has been bred to herd flocks of sheep and really needs to be on a ranch, but, a few years back, the Chikura family had received a pair from a genuine ranch in Fukushima prefecture run by the Ministry of Agriculture and Forestry. Soon after, the bitch gave birth to a litter, and one of the puppies was sent to Takane. This happened just as she and her husband were traveling to America for a month, so she begged Yuri to look after the puppy during their absence. Well aware of Yuri's aversion to dogs, she emphatically instructed her to take good care of the puppy, but when the couple returned they discovered that, in spite of those repeated instructions, he had died. Upon investigating, they learned that Yuri had tossed the puppy out of the house into the cold after subjecting him to all sorts of mistreatment. Hidako, and even her husband, Natsuyama Genzō, shed tears of pity.

From time to time, that good couple grew so exasperated that they'd decide to ask Yuri to leave, but then they would change their minds and let her stay, until at last there was another incident. It was like this: one day, over a year ago, a notice arrived that Yuri's father had died in a cave-in at the Ōmuta mine. The manner of his death was truly tragic—as he was flattened against a rock, exhausted and clinging fast to it, an iron rod pierced his head from the crown to his jaw, and a thick spike ran him through his feet, like Christ on the cross. They said he had probably died instantly. After that, it only made sense for Yuri's family to move from Kyushu back to their hometown, Osaka, and there they set up a fruit shop using the money they had received from the mining company as compensation for her father's death—over a million yen. Yuri knew she would miss Tokyo and wanted to remain with the Takane household, but was repeatedly advised otherwise by her mother, by her aunts and uncles, by Hidako and her husband, and by Raikichi and his wife—*You can't impose on Mr. Natsuyama and his wife forever*, they all said; *If you wait too long, you'll miss your chance to marry; you ought to go back home and look after your mother; in Osaka, you'd have all sorts of marriage prospects*—until at last she made up her mind and moved back in with her mother. That was last spring.

Yuri's now living with her family at their house on the bank of the Yodogawa and commutes to a job she found at a company in Osaka. She has received proposals from several gentlemen and has gone on a few marriage interviews, some offering excellent terms, I understand—almost too good for her, really—but she rejects them all, complaining, "Osaka men are so low-class!" Whatever we might think, she got used to the dashing men at the Tokyo film studios, so it's natural that she has become picky and now dreams of being the wife of a promising young assistant director. But that's never going to happen. Recently, everyone has been trying to get her to change her mind: *It's time to give up such unrealistic dreams, find a good man, and get married here in Osaka. You have all the qualities that make an ideal wife, the sort that a man would be proud to take anywhere, if only you'll give up these outsized ambitions.*

Incidentally, if, during her time in Atami, she'd already acquired such polish that she completely effaced her old appearance, then she raised her allure to another level during her two or three years working for the Takane household and moving every day in the most fashionable Tokyo society. Walking down the Ginza, she looked every inch the stylish and respectable young lady. What's more, she enjoyed all sorts of opportunities to receive gifts from Hidako. Each time the star and her husband went on a trip—to America, say, or to

France — they would give her several unusual things from the souvenirs they brought back. Her trousseau continued to grow.

This sequel has gotten rather long, so let me return to the previous story, Yuri's rivalry with Gin. If you're wondering which of them became intimate with Mitsuo first, well, it was Gin. She returned to her hometown in Kagoshima for a while after receiving word that her mother was ill. It was during that break that Mitsuo first started putting the moves on Yuri. Mitsuo, who had always taken pride in the size of his manhood, had a habit of showing it off to the opposite sex, and one day, meeting Yuri on the stone steps to the house, he'd tried this method on her, and she had shouted, "What a pervert!" — nothing in particular developed from that, though.

Gin returned from Kagoshima before long, but Mitsuo continued flirting with Yuri. At the same time, he didn't break things off with Gin, but went out with her just as before. Gin could not have been ignorant of this romantic triangle. Though Mitsuo's two girlfriends were living under one roof, they had to behave themselves in front of their master, so they just ignored the tension between them, never quarreling or coming to blows. Instead, Suzu and Koma, serving as Gin and Yuri's surrogates, competed furiously to investigate Mitsuo's movements and report back.

There were several reasons (apart from those I've already mentioned) that Yuri fell behind Gin in this competition, but above all she was defeated by Gin's tenacity. There are all sorts of anecdotes about what went on between Mitsuo and Gin, but nothing particularly interesting has been handed down about what happened between him and Yuri. If you think about their rendezvous and where they took place, they never amounted to more than driving around in his taxi or, at most, having tea together at a café.

I have one interesting story about that automobile. Even though all the other maids took the bus whenever they went into town on errands, Gin always asked permission to get a ride in Mitsuo's taxi instead. After he brought her back home to Narusawa, she would pay the fare from her own money. I've already mentioned that there are two sets of stone steps going up the hill to Shōheki Cottage. One is the path that leads to the Kōa Kannon, and the other comes out by the rear garden of the cottage. If you're approaching by the national road that runs below the house, you first pass the path to the rear garden and only after that the entrance to the Kōa Kannon path, by the rustic twig gate of Tamai Ryōhei's villa. As a rule, Gin would come halfway down this second path to lie in wait for Mitsuo. So whenever she saw Gin head down the stone steps, Koma would announce: "Yuri-san! Yuri-san! Gin's going out!" Upon hearing that, Yuri would dash down the garden steps to accost Mitsuo one step ahead of Gin. After a while whispering sweet nothings with Yuri, Mitsuo would head for the entrance to the other path to meet Gin, looking as if butter wouldn't melt in his mouth. On these occasions, it was always Gin who paid the taxi fare. Yuri really ought to have paid sometimes, but that shrewd girl never did.

Yuri's wildly boastful attitude and her rude way of speaking caused misunderstandings. Sometimes I'd hear her talking on the phone and wonder what she could be so angry about. I'm sure she behaved differently with Mitsuo, but a stranger listening to her couldn't help but think, *What a coarse woman!* It was just the way she spoke, though; she wasn't really bad at heart. She understood the principle of things, too, and, as I said before, she had an understanding nature.

Time and time again, Raikichi and his wife would tell her, "You do yourself no favors, talking that way. Don't you see? Isn't there anything you can do to break the habit?—a clever girl like you." But it seems she still hasn't reformed.

I heard that, before she met Mitsuo, she liked someone at the Tomoeya grocery store, but it didn't go well, and this was one reason for her bluster.

Mitsuo's parents were still in good health, and he had an older sister and a younger sister; they could hardly be expected to approve of Yuri's way of talking. She would put up with any hardship, if only she could be married to Mitsuo-san; she said she would take care not to say anything rude to his mother or father, and show them true filial piety—but no one took her seriously. Gin, on the other hand, inspired great trust in Mitsuo's mother. Very early on, his mother asked Gin if she would consent to an *ashi-ire* trial marriage with Mitsuo. That's right: *ashi-ire* had long been practiced in the area between Izusan and Yugawara.

Chapter Eighteen

MITSUO'S MOTHER WAS AN EXCELLENT PERSON,
kindly by nature and well regarded in the neighborhood. It seems
that she was utterly charmed by Gin, for she came to visit the Chikuras in Narusawa one day to beg a favor of Sanko. *Madam may
already have heard,* she said, *but Mitsuo has become friends with some
gamblers and even now continues to waste his time with them. His father and I have spoken to him again and again, but somehow he won't
give them up. Our whole family is worried about him. The only person
who can make him stop is Gin-san. Only she can make an honest man of
our Mitsuo, and so I beg you to consider his welfare and allow Gin-san
to join our family. If you would do that, I assure you the whole family
will cherish her. Mitsuo is a terrible philanderer, I know, and involved
with several different women, but we'll make him break things off with
all of them; and I understand that he's become quite serious with that
bus conductress, but, if you'll leave it to me, I will give her some money
to break up with him and resolve everything once and for all.*

Gin had no objection to this proposal, needless to say. Far from objecting, she was even keener than Mitsuo's mother. She vowed ardently that she would go to Mitsuo, whatever it took; of course it would be best for him to wash his hands of those gambler friends, but, regardless of that, she would rush to him; no other woman would get her claws into him—just let one try! For some reason, however, Mitsuo, who was crucial to the plan, would not make up his mind. *Please make him consent somehow! Please make him say yes!* Hands clasped and tears streaming down her cheeks, Gin beseeched Sanko. Moved by the sentiments of Gin and the mother, Sanko summoned Mitsuo and tried to persuade him, but, though cornered at last, he remained vague and evasive. Then Gin pressed Sanko tearfully to ask him once again. This pattern was repeated several times until, at last, Sanko got Mitsuo to capitulate.

In the meantime, Yuri had left to join the Takane household, so Gin and Mitsuo could meet openly without concern for her or anyone else. Mitsuo's taxi was parked at the foot of those stone steps more and more often. Now Mitsuo would sometimes move beyond the kitchen to openly enter the maids' room and lose himself in conversation with Gin. He wouldn't enter late at night, but at any hour they could meet to talk in the garden of the empty villa on the other side of the stone stairs, just as before. The Shōnan taxi drivers lived in a dormitory next to the garage, and the owner of the company and his wife slept on the second floor of the garage. Mitsuo would wait until after midnight, when the couple were asleep, and then take his taxi out of the garage and race to the foot of the stone stairs. The owner and his wife must have heard the sound of the auto as he left, but they weren't suspicious; they thought he'd been called out to some inn for a fare. Gin was constantly restless, her mind completely taken up with Mitsuo. She couldn't settle down to work, whatever she was asked to do, and she neglected even her kitchen duties. She would sneak out the kitchen door in the middle of the night until, at last, the other maids complained to Sanko: *We can't put up with it any longer; please do something about Gin-san!*

Just as Sanko was feeling that the only thing to be done was to marry Gin off, Mitsuo's father, mother, and uncle together paid a visit to the Chikura house to make a formal proposal of marriage. According to those three, Mitsuo was determined to clean up his act and start a new life and had settled completely the troublesome debt of seven hundred thousand yen. His parents and relatives had covered half the amount, but Mitsuo had worked hard to raise the other half himself—evidence that he had turned over a new leaf, they said.

As a driver, Mitsuo apparently received a monthly salary of twenty thousand yen from the taxi company, and when you added tips it amounted to sixty or seventy thousand. Of course, several maids at the inns around town favored him and would send customers his way, so he was exceptionally busy, with more fares than most. Day by day, little by little, he had set aside some of this money to repay the debts incurred by his bad habits. In March of 1958, Mitsuo accompanied Gin to Kagoshima so that her grandmother and mother could know what sort of man she was marrying; by that point the couple must have made up their minds. They stayed in Kagoshima for one week, and Gin had to do all of the translating between the Kagoshima and Atami dialects. By the end, Mitsuo had passed inspection with the grandmother and mother. As word spread around Gin's hometown of Tomari, a great crowd of their neighbors descended on the house to get a look at Mitsuo, and these people, too, approved, offering such sentiments as "Gin always did set her sights high," along with the local expression *Yoka ni se*, meaning, "What a man!"

It was decided that her grandmother and mother would travel all the way from Kagoshima to attend the wedding in Atami that fall, in October. The couple had returned from Kagoshima in March. During the seven months until the wedding Mitsuo continued to drive for Shōnan taxi while Gin remained in the Chikura household, and the tenderness of their affection was enough to inspire jealousy in those around them forced to observe it. It's said that a woman is most beautiful when she is in love, and Raikichi has never seen another woman, before or since, as beautiful as Gin was during those seven months. She had always been a beauty, but those months were special. Again and again he was struck by it—*Being in love can make someone this beautiful!* One didn't even notice the scar over her eye. And perhaps, rather than "her" beauty, we should call it "love's" beauty. It wasn't only Raikichi who harbored these feelings; Sanko, Nioko, Numeko, and Mutsuko all noticed too. "How beautiful!" Nioko would cry sometimes in admiration, and once said, "You can't know if you haven't shared the bath with her, but her skin is pure white all over—it's like nothing I've ever seen!" On Christmas Eve of the previous year, Mitsuo had given Gin a bright blue mohair cardigan that cost three thousand five hundred yen, and the color looked so fetching on her that she wore it all the time, even in the house—the image is still burned on Raikichi's mind.

Whenever he had the leisure, Raikichi would take Gin for a ride in Mitsuo's taxi to Hakone or Odawara or as far as Kamakura. When he traveled to Tokyo his companion was always Gin, though in that case, they went by train, not Mitsuo's taxi. Those trips were a pleasure; he would wander aimlessly with her around the department stores in Ginza or take her to a movie theater in Hibiya. One time, Raikichi had an appointment with a friend who lived on the street behind the Mitsukoshi Department Store in Ginza Yonchome and, when they visited the house, he purposely had the taxi stop five or six doors away and told Gin to wait in the car. When he had concluded his visit and was taking his leave, the friend walked him out to the street and, seeing Gin, teased him: "I see you're escorting a beautiful actress!" But Raikichi just smirked; rather than embarrassed, he was secretly proud. At the same time that Gin's face began to glow with a peculiar radiance, her body, too, betrayed a certain transformation: Raikichi, Sanko, and Nioko all noticed, though no one mentioned it until, one day, Numeko, visiting from Kyoto, said what they were thinking: "I think Gin has *become a woman*." None of them ventured to contradict her. As we learned later, their speculations were correct. Gin and Mitsuo held the exchange of engagement gifts on the first day of October, and at the very last moment before that, Gin finally confessed "the event" to Sanko.

She and Mitsuo had become physically intimate one night in March, just before they went to Kagoshima to meet her family. She'd met him at their usual spot on the stone steps and he had his way with her, but this being her first experience, she didn't really know just what he had done, she said. Sanko told her, "The two of you already have both your parents' permission and have just exchanged engagement gifts, so even if you have made a mistake in the short term, I won't condemn you very strongly, but if this sort of thing happens again, please inform me."

Then Gin replied, "Madam, I'm so sorry! I've done a terrible thing!" and began bawling like a child. After Sanko pressed her, she confessed that they had continued in this conduct all through the week that they'd spent at her parents' home in Kagoshima; in that region, where "provisional marriage" is practiced, parents are apparently not very strict about chaperoning.

Suzu, that other beauty among Gin's cohort, remained calm, perhaps due to her own self-confidence, and no rumors spread, but she began making eyes at Hasegawa Seizō, "the Receptionist" at the Shōgetsurō Inn. It was this Hasegawa who, through Suzu's mediation, had put together the money when Gin was seeking to raise fifty thousand yen to free Mitsuo from debt, so he and Suzu were already friendly, but she began to think seriously about him from around this time.

Suzu at first had no intention at all of getting married in Atami. She'd expected to return to her hometown of Mano, in Shiga prefecture, and marry someone selected by her parents; they had expected the same. That she didn't was thanks to Sanko's constantly telling her, "You might just as well get married in this region." Since Gin was going to Yugawara, Sanko hoped Suzu would settle nearby. Besides, she thought, it would be a shame for such a beautiful and clever girl, who had finally grown accustomed to city life, to be buried away in a farmhouse in the countryside. Raikichi was of the same mind. When the two of them went to Kyoto every spring and fall to spend half a month at the Asukai house in Kita-Shirakawa, they always took one maid with them, and it was usually Suzu. She had been born near Ōtsu, by the shore of Lake Biwa, so she was familiar with the geography of Kyoto, and she was expert at preparing various dishes in the Kyoto style, the Tokyo style, and the western style, so she was most useful to have with them on a trip. Furthermore, she liked the Asukai house. Keisuke's layout for the house had been improved upon by Numeko, so that downstairs there was a parlor lined with a sofa and chairs, and a dining-kitchen, separated only by a curtain that was usually drawn back. Suzu admired it all terribly—the cabinet with glass doors between the dining area and kitchen that you could open from either side, the gas range and oven, the stainless-steel sink, the sideboard, the electric refrigerator, the alcove for the telephone; and if, one day, she had a family of her own, she wanted to live in this sort of house and decorate it in just this way and, in her bedroom, to sleep in a bed like this one in which the young mistress of the house took her rest. *This is my ideal*—saying it became a habit with her. Knowing how she loved such fashionable, western things, Raikichi and the others were even less inclined to send her back to the countryside. Raikichi and Sanko often discussed Suzu's temperament, observing that, while most people had both strong points and weak points—that's normal, after all—Suzu was just about average in all her abilities. While each of the other maids—starting with Hatsu, and then Koma, Sada, Yuri, and Gin—had possessed some special quality that no one else could imitate, they said, each also had her undeniable faults; and, even though you could find faults in

Suzu too if you nitpicked, she had very few. On the other hand, that sort of personality wasn't very interesting, and compared to Koma, Yuri, and Gin she provided little in the way of diverting material for conversation.

Before Suzu became involved with Hasegawa, she met another man who she thought might be the one, a driver with Shōwa Taxi on Atami Road, and, thinking to marry him, she returned to Mano to get her parents' permission; but she learned that he had gone hiking with another woman in her absence, and she immediately, angrily, broke off their engagement. Her relationship with Hasegawa grew more serious thanks to the mediation of an old gardener who came to the Chikura house often and delivered Hasegawa's love letters to Suzu. Commissioned by Hasegawa, the old gardener delivered the letters unfailingly, but Suzu was a poor correspondent, unable to dash off a reply on the spur of the moment, and wrote only one letter to five of his, so that the gardener sometimes cautioned Hasegawa, "O-Suzu-san is rather coldhearted, isn't she?"

There was an obstinacy to her expressions that didn't suit Suzu; she spoke bluntly even to the opposite sex and wouldn't give an inch in an argument. I believe she fought sometimes with Hasegawa, too, and her fights didn't end with sweet nothings and flirting, like Gin's, but in quite vehement arguing back and forth. While Gin and Mitsuo's meetings occurred on the stone stairs leading to the Kōa Kannon, Suzu and Hasegawa would meet under the arbor in the Shōheki villa's rear garden and discuss their plans for the future. These two, however, kept their relationship pure through and through, avoiding Gin's sort of transgression.

To celebrate their engagement, Raikichi composed a poem, wrote it out on a display board, and presented it to Suzu:

> *Clever fisher-girl of Shiga of the lapping waves*
> *She catches and, at last, does not release*

Chapter Nineteen

THE MARRIAGES OF KIKUCHI KOTOKO (KNOWN within the Chikura household as Suzu) to Hasegawa Seizō, and of Iwamura Ginko (know as Gin) to Sonoda Mitsuo, were consecrated on October fifteenth, 1958, before the deity of Izusan Shrine. Kotoko and Seizō were married in the morning. Serving as go-betweens were the owner of the Shōgetsurō Inn and his wife, who placed great trust in Seizō. Also in attendance were the mother of the groom, who had traveled from his hometown in Gunma prefecture, his older brother and the brother's wife who lived in Izusan; his two younger brothers; Raikichi and Sanko; Asukai Nioko together with Keisuke; the bride's father and two uncles from Shiga; and so on. After the ceremony, the newlyweds hosted a simple reception in the annex, with clear soup and box lunches with sashimi: the owner of the Shōgetsurō, Raikichi, and others gave toasts.

In the afternoon, it was time for Gin and Mitsuo. The owner of Shōnan Taxi and his wife served as go-betweens. Also in attendance were the groom's parents from Yugawara; his older sister and her husband; his two younger sisters and their husbands; an aunt and uncle from his mother's side of the family; the head of the Yugawara Neighborhood Association and one neighborhood representative; Gin's grandmother and mother from Kagoshima; her youngest sister, Mariko; Raikichi and Sanko, Nioko, and so on. After the ceremony, the newlyweds held a reception at the home of the groom's uncle on his mother's side, on the east side of the stone steps leading to the shrine; it was lively and crowded with people, most of them locals.

Kotoko wore a pleated silk crepe kimono with tortoiseshell shapes arranged over a pattern of large chrysanthemums in red, pink, yellow, and other colors on a white ground. The sash was crimson, with a tortoise shell for the family crest. Ginko also wore a kimono of pleated silk crepe with an all-over pattern. It was predominately black and red on a white ground, with bold roundels of phoenixes at the right shoulder and the knees. There were also roundels in the form of chrysanthemums, paulownia, hollyhocks, and plum blossoms. The background was red at the sleeves and black at the hem, and four flower-shaped family crests were picked out in white. The placement of white detail here and there was very effective. The sash was of crimson pleated crepe, with chrysanthemums in an undulating pattern done in gold. Both outfits were rented from a beauty parlor in Atami where the brides got ready for their ceremonies. Beforehand, Gin, who cared about such things, had tearfully begged Sanko, "Please, Madam, tell them to pick out something really special for me to wear!" and so the beauty parlor manager had made a special trip to Tokyo to find a kimono in the latest fashion. Since Gin got to wear something almost brand new, her whole appearance was set off that much more beautifully, and her brilliance caught everyone's eye.

It had been decided that the Hasegawas would rent and live in a two-story house halfway up the mountain, between the Shōgetsurō Inn and Shōheki Cottage and just a few minutes from each. Since Seizō worked at the inn from the morning until past ten at night,

Kotoko continued to come to the Chikura house every day to work in the kitchen, going home after lunch and dinner. She asked them to please call her Suzu just as before, and so, after securing Seizō's consent, they did. Before long, she realized one feature of her dream life by having an electric refrigerator installed in their house. A dresser with a three-way mirror, given to her by the Chikura family, gleamed in her dressing room. Silk damask quilts from her mother in Mano were stacked up in the second-floor linen closet.

A similar dresser with three-way mirror from Raikichi and Sanko arrived at the Sonodas. Packages of splendid gifts arrived as well from Gin's parents in Kagoshima, and were set out for display at the house in Yugawara, but Mitsuo, intending to continue working for Shōnan Taxi for the time being, had rented a single room from the uncle who attended the ceremony, and the young couple were living there. In any case, Gin was already holding the belly-binding ceremony for a safe birth and distributing the traditional red beans and rice by the end of that December. The ceremony is supposed to be held five months after conception, and it was held not three months after her October wedding, so that would mean that the baby was conceived two or three months before. Raikichi and the others found it strange: if Gin and Mitsuo had just kept it to themselves, no one would have guessed that she was pregnant before the wedding, but they were actually letting the neighbors know—even to the extent of holding the belly-binding ceremony. Gin and Mitsuo had their reasons, though: old-fashioned customs like the belly-binding ceremony are still faithfully observed in that region, between Izusan and Yugawara. It's not much of a problem if it becomes known that a bride is already pregnant; it's much more important to hold the belly-binding at the proper time. And this was true in Gin's hometown back in Kagoshima, too, so both sets of parents were, surprisingly, in agreement.

Moving on, Gin retained various other customs that would seem old-fashioned to Tokyoites. Her father had died during the war from a disease contracted at the front, and every month, on the day that he died, she would eat only tea over rice for her three meals, without any side dishes at all. She strictly observed that custom. Also, as the seasons changed, when eating the fruits, vegetables, and so on of each new season for the first time that year, she would turn to face west, give a loud laugh, "Ah-hah-hah!" and say, "With this, let me live another seventy-five days!" In Tokyo, too, they say, "With this, let me live another seventy-five days!" but they don't do the laugh. Come to think of it, in the old days Hatsu used to laugh, "Ah-hah-hah," when she ate the first produce of each season, so it seems to be a set practice in the area around Kagoshima. The displaying of wedding gifts is another regional custom. Around Tokyo, one never invites in relatives and acquaintances to show off the gifts—not unless the bride is the daughter of a magnificent old family; but this is the general custom in Mitsuo's hometown and indeed of the whole Kyoto-Osaka region.

Though she kept it a secret, until the very day of the wedding, Gin was gripped by the fear that, when the big moment arrived, Mitsuo would steal away from the ceremony, and perhaps run away to Yuri. Though it sounds absurd, this anxiety does suggest that she may have intentionally gotten pregnant.

In April and May of the following year, as usual, Raikichi, Sanko, and Nioko traveled to Kyoto to see the cherry blossoms and were staying at the Asukai house in Kita-Shirakawa when, on May tenth, they received a call from Gin in Izusan with the news that she had given birth to a boy, and would they please think of a name for him? Raikichi immediately came up with three or four names, wrote them down on paper in Chinese characters and then phonetically as well, and mailed them off, but Gin called once again to say that she was sorry but none of these appealed to her, and she would like him to think of a few more. They finally settled on the name Takeshi after more than seven days.

When Gin's grandmother and mother returned to Kagoshima, her youngest sister, Mari, who had also attended the wedding ceremony, stayed behind to take Gin's place working in the kitchen. She was eighteen—five years younger than Gin. Gin must have gotten those big eyes of hers from their parents, because Mari had them too. According to Sanko, "Mari's eyes might be even more beautiful than Gin's. She's still just a child, wait a few years. Even women will be enthralled by a flirtatious glance from those eyes, I'll bet." So she said, and indeed this girl provided no little consolation for the loneliness Raikichi felt after Gin left. Almost every other day, it seemed, he was taking her to Tokyo as he had taken Gin in the past, to walk around this neighborhood or that and show her the department stores and movie theaters. Naive Mari must have wondered why this old man showed such interest in her—why he treated her with such special favor—and may perhaps have felt that he was becoming a bit of a nuisance. Deep down, Raikichi was looking forward with great anticipation to that time "a few years hence," when her eyes would gain the liquid sparkle, and her skin the pale sheen, of her older sister's, but, alas, she didn't stay with the Chikura household that long. To hear Gin tell it, her mother had come to regret letting her move so far away. Although she'd made the trip from Kagoshima to see her first grandchild, Takeshi, when he was born, Gin's grandmother had been too old to endure another such long trip, and it occurred to the mother that she was getting older herself and might not be able to make many more trips to see her grandchildren. Wishing that she hadn't let her darling eldest daughter marry someone so far away and wanting her youngest daughter, at least, to marry and settle nearby, she decided to summon Mari back home before she met anyone special. It was for this reason, then, that Mari returned to her hometown after only a year. Still, if Raikichi hadn't treated her with such excessive partiality, perhaps the girl wouldn't have run away in such a hurry.

At the end of April of the following year, 1960, Sanko sent Gin a banner in the shape of a carp for Takeshi's first Boys Festival, and Raikichi sent a set of toy armor and a helmet of the sort displayed at home for the festival. Since Mitsuo and Gin were living in a rented room, they brought the gifts to Mitsuo's parents' house in Yugawara and displayed them there. When Raikichi went to see the display a few days before the festival, a bamboo pole had been erected behind the house, by the bridge over the weir along the Chitose river, and from it red carp and black carp, big and small, were flapping and fluttering beside Sanko's banner.

That same year and month, Chikura Mutsuko was married to Sagara Michio, the second son of the head of an established school of Noh performers, with the ceremony and reception held at the Hotel New Japan. Mutsuko was already thirty-two years old. Her brother Keisuke's wife, Numeko, had gotten married at the age of twenty-three and given birth to their daughter Miyuki at twenty-four; because she was married to Mutsuko's elder brother, she was technically the "elder sister," but Mutsuko was actually a year older, so instead of referring to each other as "elder sister" and "younger sister," they simply used their names. In May, the newlyweds Mutsuko and Michio held a second reception at the Fujiya Hotel for the Chikura family's Atami friends and acquaintances. There were no more than ten guests—the elder brother of the late Asukai Jirō, who had been a viscount before the war; the widow of the former editor of *The Oriental Review;* Raikichi's physician, Dr. Nagasawa; the proprietress of the Tōrikyō Inn; and, with his wife, the master of the Tomoeya Inn, who had served as Sada's go-between. In addition, seated at the foot of the table were Sada with her two children, Suzu with her husband Hasegawa, Gin and Mitsuo, and then—still unmarried, and attending in her position as the senior maid in the Chikura household—Koma.

Suzu came even though she was now, two years after Gin, seven months pregnant, and big enough to draw attention. She wanted to see the "young lady" of the house, with whom she had shared her daily life for almost seven years (and who, though three years older, was only now marrying), in formal dress; also she hadn't had a chance to eat fine western cuisine in quite a long time, and had begged Seizō to invite her along.

In February of the following year, 1961, Gin gave birth to a second son. As before, she asked Raikichi to choose the boy's name, and when he proposed the name Mitsuru, it was adopted without a murmur. The older boy, Takeshi, who was now three (by the old way of reckoning age), called Raikichi "Grandpa! Grandpa!" and adored him as though he were really his grandfather. It was clear that he and the younger boy, Mitsuru, took after their mother, for they both had big, shining eyes.

It was in April of that year that the last remaining girl of that set, Koma, made a good match. Although Hatsu had been in the Chikura household's service for twenty years, give or take, starting in 1936, her total time actually at the Chikura house was not as long as that suggests, since she had returned to her hometown for several stretches over those years—during the war, when her mother fell ill, and on other occasions. Koma, on the other hand, had worked at the house continuously for thirteen years without going home once, so her total time in service may have been longer. And she was perhaps the best of all the maids, in the sense that she worked in such perfect good faith, hoping to contribute to the happiness of the entire Chikura family. Raikichi and his wife remembered with particular gratitude how, during the fifty days from November to December of 1960, when Raikichi was hospitalized at the Tokyo University hospital after a heart attack, she stayed beside him in his hospital room, constantly nursing him. There was not a single person among the doctors, the nurses—even the patients in the rooms nearby—who did not praise her.

She was thirty-two the year she got married, one year younger than Mutsuko and the same age as Numeko. Her match was a man by the name of Kashimura, born at the foot of Mount Fuji in a place celebrated for its waterfall, who had previously worked as a driver for Shōwa Taxi in the Atami Road. Fine-looking, with a dignified air, he spoke very well when called upon to do so—logically and wisely—so that before long he was chosen as the general secretary of the Shōwa

Taxi labor union. Before long, his abilities garnered greater recognition, and he advanced to the much longer title of Vice Chairman of the Executive Committee of the Shizuoka Regional Chapter of the National Automobile Transportation Workers Union. Of course, this was not a first marriage for Kashimura. He had decided to divorce his first wife in order to marry Koma.

He knew that Koma was eccentric and had many strange habits; perhaps he was attracted to her all the more because, with her strange ways, she was nevertheless such an exceptionally kind person.

Kashimura repeatedly told Raikichi and the others, "No one but me can really understand Koma-san; she's so unusual." Unfortunately, the Chikura family could not turn out for the ceremony because it was held in April, when they traveled to Kyoto for the cherry blossoms, but the customary three-times-three exchange of cups was held at the Imamiya Shrine at Sakuragaoka, and the reception was in the annex there. One day, after returning from Kyoto, Raikichi asked Koma her impressions.

"How about it? How's it feel? Is it going smoothly?"

"Marriage is really rather pleasant, isn't it," she replied. "If it's this pleasant, I should have done it much sooner." It was such a Koma-like thing to say, everyone laughed about it afterward.

Gin and Mitsuo finally vacated the room they'd been renting at his uncle's house on the approach to Izusan Gongen Shrine and returned to his parents' Yugawara home at the end of spring, 1961. Mitsuo had continued to drive for Shōnan Taxi, but at this point he quit as he'd planned to do and decided to help his father start some sort of business from the Yugawara house. The father had been running a cheap restaurant, but it was small and run down, with few customers anyway and small profits, and had never really taken off. This time, after consulting with the young couple, he completely remodeled the first floor, setting up a souvenir shop in the front and a bar in the back. Since the father had lived in the neighborhood for such a long time, he was able to secure most of the necessary capital with a loan from the bank. The shop opened on April 25. As for the shop's name, once again Raikichi was tasked with christening it, and he came up with "Shungindō," or "Spring Song," incorporating a homonym for Gin's name.

While she was at it, Gin said that she wanted him to think of a poem to put on the shop curtain, so Raikichi composed the following:

At Shungindō in Yugawara, customers without cease
On days of blowing cherry blossoms and days of glowing autumn leaves

But again Gin asked him for a revision: Around here, mandarins sell well in the fall, so instead of the line "*days of glowing autumn leaves*," can't you compose something about mandarins? How about "*days of ripening mandarins*"? That's not bad, it was decided, and so Sanko wrote out the following with her calligraphy brush, to be sent to the dyer making the curtain:

At Shungindō in Yugawara, customers without cease
On days of blowing cherry blossoms and days of ripening mandarins

Chapter Twenty

WHEN YOU PEEK INTO THE SOUVENIR SHOP AT YUGA-
wara these days to have a look, there are two sheets of colored paper
framed and hung on the back wall. On one is written the following:

> *To the mistress of Shungindō—*
> *A young wife raised in Kagoshima*
> *Selling souvenirs in the hot-spring town of Yugawara*

The other also begins "*To the mistress of Shungindō,*" and continues:

> *Who came as a bride from the port of Tomari in Satsuma Bay;*
> *She rinses her black hair in the waters of Yugawara hot spring*

Raikichi wrote these out and gave them to Gin to celebrate the success of Shungindō, where she is now the proprietress. Mitsuo's parents are not very old yet, but they've turned most of the work over
to the young couple and now live a life of ease. The father, who got

used to handling fish in the days when he ran his takeout business, enjoys going out to fish early in the morning, upstream on the Chitose river that flows behind their house. He often catches sweetfish and trout and has Gin or Mitsuo carry them in water, still alive, up to the Chikura house.

Raikichi likes rice porridge made with sweetfish, and for that you need the live fish, which is difficult enough to find in Kyoto, never mind the mountains of Izusan, but in the morning, before breakfast, a telephone call will come from Gin to say "We're sending over some fresh fish now!" and before long either Mitsuo or Gin will turn up, leading Takeshi by the hand or carrying Mitsuru piggyback, bringing a bowl filled with sweetfish swimming around in water. They have Mitsuo's father to thank for this luxury. Trout is another of Raikichi's favorites, and the flavor of a big, fresh, lively trout is something special. Whenever Raikichi imagines the old man casting his line into the rapids of the Chitose river and pulling in such trophies, Schubert's lied "Die Forelle" comes to his mind.

Mitsuo's mother is very good at making simmered red beans and sometimes when she prepares a batch, she packs some into a set of stacked lacquer boxes or an enamel tin and sends her son or his wife over with it. Even before she married Mitsuo, Gin had heard people say, "There aren't many mothers as good as that one; it'll be a lucky girl who marries into that family!" and now she knows it to be true. The mother doesn't interfere with the shop at all but entrusts everything to Gin, devoting herself entirely to looking after her two grandchildren. There's little for Mitsuo to do in the shop, either, since the customers are mainly hot-springs visitors, and Gin handles everything, from greeting customers to keeping the accounts. At some point, she took over management of the whole household.

Sometimes, seeing Gin as she is now, Sanko will talk to Raikichi about the old days. When Gin was working in their house, there was not another maid so difficult and troublesome. Once she fell for Mitsuo, she directed all her energies toward him: neglecting her duties in the kitchen, she would steal away for a break and spend it at her dresser, making up her face. She never once allowed even the tip of her nose to become shiny—that's why she always looked so beautiful in those days. She inconvenienced the other maids, arousing extraordinary resentment. But that didn't trouble her. The most selfish of all the maids, with her unwavering arrogance and obstinacy—but wasn't it remarkable that, by persisting in her selfishness till the very end, she was able to defeat all her rivals? By patient persuasion, she had convinced Mitsuo to completely correct all his former faults one by one—his gambling, womanizing, spending time at the tracks, his pile of debts, and so on—no one else could have accomplished that. *I'll make an honest man of Mitsuo,* she had tearfully vowed to Sanko, *if only I'm allowed to be with him*; and she had done it—something impossible for anyone but her. "Only Gin can do it," Mitsuo's mother had said, and she had been right.

"Gin really does possess the indomitable passion of a Kagoshima woman, overcoming every obstacle to get what she wants, no matter what it takes—she's remarkable!"

"Looking back on it now, all the selfishness that we put up with seems rather like a mark of her special affection."

Little Takeshi—and only he—has free access to Raikichi's study. Whenever Mitsuo or Gin brings him over, the boy runs immediately to Raikichi's desk, calling "Grandpa!"

"Look who's here! Takeshi!" Raikichi will lead him into the corridor, saying, "Do we have any cake or something for this little guy?" Grabbing a few sweet buns for the dog and telling the maid to bring the cake, he takes the boy out to the dog house in the garden. There he spends a pleasant twenty or thirty minutes with the boy and his mother or father, playing with the dog.

Raikichi has three grandchildren, the children of his daughter by his first wife, but that daughter followed her mother to Tokyo and married there, so Raikichi seldom sees the children. Sanko has two grandchildren from her previous marriage, but one lives in Kyoto and the other in Tokyo, so you couldn't say that they see these children often, either. Raikichi would like to live where he could gaze at the face of Numeko's daughter, Miyuki, from morning till evening, but health issues make him reluctant to move to Kyoto with its poor climate. At his age—seventy-seven, by the old way of reckoning—he has to be content with visiting the Kita-Shirakawa house twice a year, spring and fall, for ten days to two weeks. Raikichi had disliked children in his youth and originally took little interest in his progeny, but he has gradually come to understand their charm and become expert at soothing them—a sure sign that he is getting old. Whenever he sees Takeshi come bursting into his study calling "Grandpa!" and giving him a hug, Raikichi forgets that the boy is not in fact his own grandson, and wants to do all he can for him.

It isn't just Takeshi. His brother, Mitsuru, is dear to Raikichi too; and Suzu's son, Tamotsu, is dear; and Koma's little boy, Tadasu, born just this past April. Having lost all affection for his hometown, Tokyo, and with no plans to return to that native ground, Raikichi looks forward to watching these children grow up, and relying on their mothers as he would his own daughters. However, since Hasegawa Seizō left the Shōgetsurō to go work at the Ōsaki Hotel, moving from Narusawa to Yugawara, Gin's house is the closest, and her sons come to visit more often than anyone else, bringing with them, as usual, sweetfish or trout, or red beans. I suppose Raikichi's life won't change much from here on in, and so he's likely to live out his final years in this fashion. Among all the maids who looked after the Chikura family, and were looked after by them in turn, only these three, Gin, Suzu, and Koma, remained in the area even after marrying and starting a family and still come to visit Raikichi. They're all still young, so there's no knowing how they might change, but at least Gin's family is unlikely to move away, since they've been living in the area and running businesses there for two generations now. Raikichi hopes that's the case.

The first maid that Raikichi and his wife employed after they took their first house in the Hanshin area was the Kagoshima-born Hatsu, and after that there were several more from the town of Tomari, including Etsu, Ume, Setsu, Gin, and Mari, each leaving behind an unforgettable impression, so that Raikichi came to hold a special affection for Kagoshima though he had never visited the place. Those former maids often said, "Come visit, Sensei; we'll give you a warm welcome!" but, even as he thought, *Yes, I'll do that when I have the chance*, he had slipped somehow into old age. Times had changed. Even now, unable to forget the old days of Hatsu and Ume, he occasionally sends a letter to Kagoshima asking them to recommend a "helper," but the girls today can all find better conditions working in offices or factories, and very few want to enter service; even if one does come once in a while, she never settles down for long, but stays for one year and then returns home. Hatsu stayed for twenty years, and Koma, from Kyoto, for thirteen. Even Gin stayed for four or five, but that sort of thing is a dream of the past now. Today's girls stay for six months or a year, thinking it good training for married life, then they hear from home about a marriage prospect, and they're gone.

That reminds me: there's something that I've neglected to write about because the opportunity hasn't arisen, and I'd like to note it here. The fact of the matter is, Raikichi loves Japanese-style massage, and whenever he grows stiff from working, without fail, he gets his legs rubbed, usually during his afternoon nap. Since he detests moxibustion treatment, it's either acupuncture or massage, and he wouldn't receive acupuncture treatment from anyone but a real master. With massage, if it is a real specialist in massage therapy, they're apt to go on too long, massaging him until he wakes up, and so, to unknot his stiffened joints properly, it's best to ask one of the maids to give him a rub. Of course, it requires certain qualifications. First of all, that person has to have an understanding of pressure points. Second, her fingertips have to be plump, fleshy, and soft—this is more important than you might think. Some professional masseuses reputed for their skill have hard, painful fingertips and, as for that, no thank you! Furthermore, Raikichi prefers to lie face down, on his belly, and be rubbed hard from his buttocks up to the vertebrae of his lower back. Sometimes, he'll have the masseuse sit right down heavily on his lower back. Once that's finished, he'll have her stand with the soles of her feet pressing down on the soles of his feet. When he doesn't receive this treatment, he can't help but feel unsatisfied.

The most talented at this had been Hatsu. To be mounted by the full weight of that ample woman and trod on by her great feet, with their beautiful, lily-white soles—that had been a genuine pleasure. After Hatsu, the one with the softest hands and feet had been Yuri. However, although there was no objection to her in terms of her body, she'd complained so much as she worked on him, and seemed to be so put out, that he would lose interest and stop her. Suzu and Koma would do it if asked, but both had the defect of thin, hard fingertips. As for Gin, the softness of her fingertips was ideal, but Raikichi had always been rather reserved when she massaged him— perhaps because of her beauty.

Not long ago, another maid came to work for a short time, a girl from Ibaraki prefecture named "Mie-san" (by this time, we were us- ing the polite "-san" with the maids). Her hands and her feet were extremely soft and white, but, unfortunately, she returned to her hometown last fall, and now there's not one maid in the household who's good at giving a massage.

Well then, it's about time to draw this long chronicle to a close. Mind you, various young women have come to take care of things in the kitchen more recently, thanks to a classified ad in the *Weekly Shinchō*, and so Raikichi and the others have not been inconve- nienced, I am happy to say. In fact, many of the applicants are proper young ladies from good homes. These women are what is now called "helpers," however, not the "maids" of old, so it wouldn't do to in- clude them in this chronicle.

Raikichi turned seventy-seven on July 24 of this year. On the Sat- urday, the twenty-eighth, at five o'clock in the afternoon, a simple birthday banquet was held for only his closest associates at the Fujiya Hotel in town—a very quiet affair, not at all ostentatious. Only his most intimate friends and family were invited. For entertainment, the koto master Tomiyama Seikin and his wife performed the song "Forgetting the Capital," and "The Tea Song"; Mutsuko's husband, Sagara Michio, performed the Noh dance "Kagekiyo"; Asukai Miyuki danced "A List of Pines" in the style of the Inoue school of Kyoto dance; and so on. In addition, Raikichi issued invitations to those former maids with whom, since 1935, he had enjoyed an especially close connection, and they came from far and wide to Atami on the seventh of August and had a second banquet starting at six that evening, in the Japanese-style room upstairs at the Chinese restaurant Peking, in the city. Joining the party were, first of all, Nakanobu and his wife, who set up the bookstore with the wide storefront by the bus stop near Kyoto University, on Higashi-Ichijō Avenue in Ushinomiya-cho, in the Yoshida section of Kyoto. Then there was Hatsu, who'd married into a farming family outside Wakayama. Bringing two of her children with her, she stopped on the way to meet up with her younger brother, Kichie, who lived in Kobe, and then, inviting Ume to join them, arrived on the afternoon of the sixth, the day before the banquet. Ume also brought two children with her, so all together they made a lively party of seven.

Meeting Ume again for the first time in more than ten years, Raikichi and Sanko were surprised by her brisk manner of speech, utterly unchanged from before. Needless to say, she had entirely recovered from her past unfortunate affliction, of which there remained not a trace. Raikichi and Sanko had reserved rooms for all seven at an inn near the Shungindō in Yugawara, and I'm sure that night those old friends, all born and raised in Tomari and now unexpectedly reunited under one roof, reveled in the atmosphere of the "Prefectural Association" of old. Next was Sada, mistress of a sushi shop in Zushi, and her two children. Then Suzu and her husband, Hasegawa Seizō, and their eldest boy, Tamotsu. Then Gin and her husband, Sonoda Mitsuo, and their two boys, Takeshi and Mitsuru. Then Koma and her husband Kashimura Tsuneo, and their eldest boy, Tadasu. Others rushed over to join the party—the Kyoto dry-goods saleswoman, Katō, with whom many of them were close during their time as maids, the master of the little restaurant Wakana on the beach in Atami, and more. Five joined from the family's side: Raikichi and Sanko, Asukai Nioko, and Sagara Mutsuko and her son Tsutomu. For the entertainment, Nakanobu, a man with a lovely voice and some experience in the Noh drama, recited a passage from the play *Takasago*; Kato performed the monologue "The Watermelon Thief"; Mitsuo got everyone to sing along to "Cute Baby"; and, to finish, the night's special attraction: the master of Wakana danced "The Chieftain's Daughter" to loud acclaim.

"Everyone, please lend me your hands," said the master of Wakana, taking the lead. "To Sensei's health: *Banzai*!"

And he heard them clap three times: *shan, shan, shan*.

Afterword

ISHŌAN, OR "THE HERMITAGE OF THE LEANING pine," stands on the west bank of the Sumiyoshi River in the cosmopolitan Hanshin region, which stretches between the cities of Osaka and Kobe in western Japan, bordered by the ocean to the south and green mountains to the north. The small house, now a museum, received its poetic name from Tanizaki Junichiro (1886–1965), who lived there with his wife, Matsuko, and her sisters from 1936 until 1943 and made it a setting for both his best-loved novel, *The Makioka Sisters* (*Sasameyuki*), which depicts the cultured and leisurely world of the prewar bourgeoisie, and for his last novel, *The Maids*. While signs throughout the house recall for visitors scenes from the earlier work, however, and promotional materials advertise it as "the *Makioka Sisters* house," there is little mention of the later novel, which describes the same world in a lighter, comic mode and from the perspective not of the pampered family but of the maids who served them. Yet that later work, translated here, though it may not draw as many tourists to Ishōan, is an entertaining and important complement to the author's earlier works. It gives us a more complete picture of that prewar world—a picture in which issues of class are brought to the fore. It also gives us a fuller sense of Tanizaki's career, as he reviews it in his last years, and of the themes that preoccupied this giant of Japanese letters.

The Maids was originally serialized in the weekly *Sunday Mainichi* in 1962 and published as a book the following year. The original title, *Daidokoro Taiheiki*, refers to a fourteenth-century work, the *Taiheiki*, or "Chronicle of the Great Peace," which, despite its title, is the historical record of a war between the courts of two rival claimants to the imperial throne. A "*daidokoro*" is a kitchen. The novel relates the stories of several maids who work in the household of Chikura Raikichi and his wife Sanko between 1935 and 1962, a turbulent period that witnessed the rise of fascism in Japan and the militarization of everyday life, the war years, defeat and occupation, and postwar recovery. During that period, the family first settles in Kobe, then moves to rural Atami in the east to escape the air bombing of Japan's cities. After the war, they divide their time between Atami and various houses in Kyoto. By the end of the novel, they have made Atami their main home.

The novel serves as a "below stairs" companion to the "above stairs" stories related in such earlier works as *The Makioka Sisters*. The interactions between master and servant are more physically intimate, though, than those familiar to us from novels, films, and television series about British country life, where the service stairs connect and separate two distinct spheres. Ishōan, which served as the model for Raikichi and Sanko's first house together, comprises only about sixteen hundred square feet over two floors, with no basement; the maids would have shared a small room next to the kitchen measuring only about sixty-six square feet. They and the family would therefore have been on top of one another much of the time. This proximity helps to explain Raikichi's close observation of the maids and their daily lives—why he has so many opportunities to critique their hygiene or examine their penmanship. A strict class hierarchy polices that proximity through the end of the war but, over the span of the story, we witness the democratization of postwar society reflected in the master-servant relationship until, by the end of the novel, the class structure has relaxed enough for the toddler son of a former maid to call Raikichi "Grandpa."

The novel's long look back at Japan's recent history also constitutes a fictionalized retrospective of the second half of Tanizaki's life. Tanizaki inserted himself into many of his works. The situation of Teinosuke in *The Makioka Sisters*, for example, mirrors the author's own: living near the Sumiyoshi river with the second of four daughters of an Osaka merchant family. In *The Maids*, too, the head of the household has much in common with his author. Raikichi's age and birthday are the same as Tanizaki's (chapter 20). He is an author and suffers from wartime censorship as Tanizaki did with *The Makioka Sisters* (chapter 4). The house by the Sumiyoshi River is not the only address they share; like Raikichi, Tanizaki lived in Atami, relocated to Kyoto, and then returned to Atami, remaining there until 1964, when he moved to Yugawara. Chapter 16 details Raikichi's friendship with a movie star named "Takane Hidako" and nicknamed "Dako-chan," a barely veiled reference to one of Japan's greatest stars, Takamine Hideko, known to fans as "Deko-chan." Tanizaki got to know Takamine during the filming of the first screen adaptation of *The Makioka Sisters*, in which she starred as the youngest sister, Taeko. Extending the reference, the novel gives "Dako-chan's" husband the name "Natsuyama Genzō," while the real-life Deko-chan's husband was Matsuyama Zenzō. The author indulges in more playful self-referentiality when he mentions that one of the maids owns a complete set of Tanizaki's translation of *The Tale of Genji*, poking fun at his own mass appeal. In the classist, sexist, sensualist Raikichi, the novel presents Tanizaki's parodic self-portrait.

The Maids also offers a new perspective on the east-west tensions that energize so much of Tanizaki's work. The author's career is defined in several ways by his 1923 move from Tokyo, in the Kantō region (that is, the eastern part of Japan's main island, Honshū), to the Kansai region in the west, which encompasses the ancient imperial capital Kyoto, the merchant capital Osaka, and the cosmopolitan city of Kobe. Tanizaki was born a true Edokko, or "child of Edo," the term for those who trace their roots to the commoner class of that city before 1868, the year that the Meiji emperor relocated his court there, rendering it "Tokyo" (the "Eastern capital") and ushering in an era of modernization. Tanizaki was born and raised in that modern national capital. His early career manifested a fascination with modernity and the west, most notably in his 1924 novel *Naomi* (*Chijin no ai*), in which the narrator, Jōji, details his obsession with a "modern girl" and Mary Pickford lookalike. Tanizaki pursued this fascination beyond his writing, too, moving to a house in nearby Yokohama, designed and furnished in western style.

The Great Kantō Earthquake of 1923, which destroyed much of Tokyo, brought that life to an end. Tanizaki relocated to the Kansai region, living at various locations in Kyoto and Kobe, and immediately began to report back to his readers in the capital about life in this region with its distinct dialect, cuisine, and cultural traditions. His early essays from this period are tinged with scorn for his new surroundings. For example, "Travels in the Hanshin Region" ("Hanshin kenbunroku"), published in the literary journal *Bungei shunjū* in 1925, begins, "Osakans are a race of people who, as a matter of course, allow their children to urinate on the floor while riding a train. Tokyoites will be surprised to hear this, but I assure you I am not making it up." Quickly, though, he warms to the region and its people, and by 1929 he declares in the essay "At Okamoto" ("Okamoto nite") that he will never return to live in Tokyo again. Meanwhile, he begins to chronicle the local people and customs in his novels.

This interest in Kansai is wrapped up with Tanizaki's vaunted "return to Japan." As daily life was militarized and government censors pressured writers to celebrate "national spirit," Tanizaki evinced a new interest in traditional Japanese culture that led him to translate the eleventh-century classic *The Tale of Genji* into contemporary Japanese (1939–41) and to reinterpret a traditional tale in *A Portrait of Shunkin* (*Shunkinshō*, 1933). This "return" also produced essays for the popular press, most notably *In Praise of Shadows* (*In'ei raisan*, 1933), in which Tanizaki explores (not without irony) a self-orientalization and exoticization of the past to counter or supplement the influence of a western modernity.

As part of this "return," Tanizaki sometimes tended to reduce the Kyoto-Osaka-Kobe region to a nostalgic tradition set against the modernity of the imperial capital. In the essay *Osaka and its People as I See Them* (*Watakushi no mita Ōsaka oyobi Ōsakajin*, 1932), for example, he writes, "While the petit bourgeoisie of Tokyo, caught up in the currents of the times, seem to be swept to destruction one after another, in Osaka one frequently encounters small businessmen still stubbornly holding their ground. Walking the old-fashioned narrow streets in such quarters as Senba, one cannot but notice the sheer number of family-operated businesses defying the powerful tides of large-scale capitalism." At the same time, he acknowledged (or asserted) his position as outsider, writing that "I will probably never lose my natural disposition as a Tokyoite, and so my observations will, after all, always be made through the eyes of an 'immigrant from Tokyo.'"*

By the end of *The Maids*, we may wonder if Tanizaki can still claim outsider status. His alter ego Raikichi slips unwittingly into Kansai dialect, using words and phrases unintelligible to Tokyoites. Meanwhile, the maids introduce a new pole to his map of Japan:

---

* Translation in Ken Ito, *Visions of Desire: Tanizaki's Fictional Worlds* (Stanford, CA: Stanford University Press, 1991).

Kagoshima in the extreme west, from which most of them come. The narrator describes the maids in the ethnographic manner with which, in earlier works, Tanizaki detailed the people, the speech, and the customs of Kyoto, Osaka, and Kobe. Their dialect, for example, is like the "jabbering of southern barbarians." The addition of Kagoshima allows Tanizaki and his readers a new perspective on Kansai, from which it begins to look like a center.

•

I am deeply grateful to Keith Vincent for his generous invitation to make this translation, to Tomoyuki Sasaki for his invaluable assistance in its completion, and to Kathe Cronin for her careful reading.

MICHAEL P. CRONIN

NOTES ON THE TRANSLATION

All names are given in Japanese style, surname first and given name second. The original work gives all years in Japanese style, numbered from the beginning of each new imperial reign. These have been converted to the Gregorian calendar in the translation.